DEATH RUN

DEATH RUN

by JIM MURPHY

CLARION BOOKS
TICKNOR & FIELDS: A HOUGHTON MIFFLIN COMPANY
NEW YORK

Clarion Books
Ticknor & Fields, a Houghton Mifflin Company
Copyright © 1982 by Jim Murphy
Printed in the United States of America.

Library of Congress Cataloging in Publication Data
Murphy, Jim, 1947– Death run.
Summary: An incident in a park leads to an accidental death,
but a police detective wonders if it was an accident—or murder.
[1. Mystery and detective stories. 2. Death—Fiction]
I. Title. PZ7.M9535De [Fic] 81-10265
ISBN 0-89919-065-0 AACR2

To my parents, Helen and Jim Murphy,
for their constant encouragement and love

1

---

*B*rian had been sitting on the rail fence long enough for the uneven edge to pinch off circulation in his buttocks, sending a tingling numbness down his legs. He shifted position. This gave him a few moments' relief, but then the loss of sensation continued to spread. Once again he slid from the fence and stamped his feet until normal blood flow returned.

As he went through this action—was it the fourth or fifth time?—the sun dipped behind the trees and a chilly dusk took hold, intensifying his uneasy feeling.

Take it slow, he told himself, switching from stamping to rocking from one foot to the other. Roger had said it might take him a while to get there. He had to pick up a muffler clamp or something for his car, and Al was going along with him. And you could never tell when Sticks might show up.

With only a quick glance around, Brian eased himself onto the lowest rail of the fence and thrust his hands into his jacket pockets. It was an awkward angle to sit at, but the rail was rounder, softer on his rear end. He scanned the park again for his friends.

Van Bedford Park wasn't very large—two hundred yards long, a hundred wide. Directly across from Brian, near the main entrance, were the basketball and tennis courts. Next to them was a flat, treeless expanse used for baseball, football, and soccer. Brian could just make out the faint chalk-mark remains of the various playing fields.

Brian was in the small, rectangular picnic area, empty now except for a few leafless birch trees. To his back, circling the entire park and shielding it from the surrounding factories, was an uncared-for woods. Brian was sure this was where Roger had told him to wait. But aside from a few guys shooting baskets, the place was empty.

Clouds inched in after the sun set and caused the darkness to deepen and play tricks with Brian's vision. He focused his eyes on the basketball players and was able to count three—no, four—on the court. Dark, featureless shapes, bouncing, juking and weaving as they ran a series of plays. At this distance he couldn't hear the ball being dribbled or the frantic squeak of sneakers or the players' shouts—a silence that made the action seem flawless. He felt his tension draining away, and as that happened, Amy's face materialized, smiling and warm. . . . That's the way she'd been today when he'd broken their date for the night. She'd simply smiled and said, "No problem. I've got an older brother so I understand about boys' night out." She was always so understanding; it made Brian feel guilty.

A rustling movement startled Brian. His head swung around and he discovered, inches from his face, a huge, distorted white mass—a face—staring at him, grinning hideously. Brian's head and body snapped away from the vision, his heels slid on the grass, and he fell off his perch, his head bouncing against a fence rail as he came down.

"Boo!" a voice said, followed by a familiar high-pitched cackling. Brian looked up and found Sticks standing next to him.

"Why'd you do that? Huh?" With his hands in his pockets, Brian had landed on the damp ground and fallen over like a sack of potatoes. He pushed himself into a sitting position and felt his skull for blood. More angrily, he added, "You could've killed me!"

"You were on another planet, Halihan. Deep space." Straight blond hair fell into Sticks' eyes as more laughter overcame him. "I could have driven a tank in here and you wouldn't have noticed."

"You wouldn't think it was so funny . . ."

2

"Take it easy. It was only a little joke."

"What if there was a nail sticking out of the fence?" Brian patted the back of his head and found a painful lump forming.

"Don't go and get bent out of shape," Sticks said. "Okay, I'm sorry. Here, give me your hand."

He grabbed Brian's hand even though Brian hadn't offered it and pulled him to his feet. Then, as if nothing had happened, he began telling Brian about the explosion his oddball chem teacher had accidentally set off that day.

Sticks was a strange one, all right, his moods always shifting. Open and friendly one moment, the next quiet, withdrawn. Today he seemed playful, and that put Brian a little at ease. As a sophomore and the youngest, Brian was the target of most of Sticks' jokes.

Brian tried to ignore Sticks as much as possible by concentrating on cleaning leaves from his jacket. Disregarding Sticks wasn't easy, especially since he punctuated his own story with bursts of uncontrolled laughter. This time Brian heard the approaching footsteps, and when he looked he saw Roger and Al moving through the trees about fifty feet away.

"How's the car doing?" Sticks asked.

A wave of jealousy swept over Brian. For some reason, he had wanted to be the first to say something to Roger.

"Muffler's shot," Roger called back. "It'll be out of commission for a while." Then Roger hurled his six-foot frame over the fence in a single graceful motion. "What's going on here anyway?" Roger asked as he approached. "We heard your hyena whoop a mile away."

Al followed him over the fence. He was half a head shorter, chunkier, and wore a khaki-colored raincoat that caught on a post when he tried to imitate Roger's vault.

Sticks said, "Must have been when I spooked Halihan here. Snuck right up next to him and—powee—he was airborne. It was great."

3

"For him it was great," Brian mumbled.

Roger came up to the two, looking first at Sticks and then at Brian. Brian's scowl was more embarrassed than angry.

"You ought to treat this man better," Roger said. "He's been on an important mission for us." He turned to Brian. "Right?"

"Right," Brian said, remembering the beer. He leaned over the fence, pulled the six-pack out hurriedly, and broke a can from the plastic carrying band. "They're sixteen ounces too," he said, handing one to Roger. "MacPheason leaves them near the door."

"You mean that old coot didn't scream murder?" Roger tore the aluminum tab open and a jet of foam shot into the air, swirled, and landed on the front of Sticks' jacket. Roger flashed Brian a quick smile and took a long gulp before handing the can to Al.

"I waited until he went into the back room," Brian explained. "He watches game shows most of the time, so it was easy." Sticks looked up from wiping foam off his jacket and Brian tossed him a can.

Brian never failed to admire the way Roger handled things. Always calm and self-assured, always weighing his actions carefully. He probably picked some of that up from his father, a partner in a New York law firm. But it seemed natural with Roger. Like just now. Without making a big deal of it, he'd taken some of the steam out of Sticks and even made getting the beer sound important.

Sticks drank some beer and ran the back of his hand across his mouth. He wasn't about to share his with anyone, so Brian tore another can off for himself and popped it open.

"So what are we going to do?" Roger asked. "Without my car we're on foot, and it's supposed to get a lot colder tonight."

Al hunkered into a tight ball and pulled his raincoat around him tightly. He drank some beer and handed the can back to Roger. Al said, "I don't care what we do as long as it's cheap."

"We could hang around the bowling alley," Sticks suggested, "and watch fat ladies bowl."

Roger moaned and shook his head. "You can't do anything in there without the manager jumping all over you."

"Besides," Al said, "it always smells like floor polish. Makes me sneeze."

"We could go to a dance," Brian said hesitantly. He took a quick swig of beer and realized the back of his head had stopped hurting. He belched loudly.

"Real stylish, Halihan," Sticks said sarcastically.

"What about this dance?" Roger asked.

Brian said, "There's a mixer at the girls' academy on Park Street at eight or eight-thirty. I saw it in the paper."

"Does it cost?" This from Al, who in the fading light seemed like a large rock covered with moss.

"I don't know," Brian said, shrugging. "There might be some kind of admission. A dollar maybe."

"I've got a little money," Roger said. "We could do worse than spend Friday with a bunch of females. Is that the Catholic school?"

"Yeah. St. Teresa's, I think."

A mischievous smile spread across Roger's face. "Hungry Catholic females, no less. Sounds good to me. What about the rest of you?"

"Fine by me," Sticks said, draining his can of beer and tossing it into the tall grass. "Maybe we can fix Halihan up with some honey."

"Brian's already doing okay in that department," Roger said. "Aren't you?"

"Sure." Brian thought of Amy again and felt himself blushing. He was thankful for the darkness.

"Maybe you can give me some pointers, Halihan," Sticks said, nudging him playfully. "Hey, did I tell you guys what happened in my chem class? It was great. Just great."

As quickly as that, Sticks began retelling his story, complete

5

with dramatic arm gestures and sound effects. This time, Brian listened to the details, was even able to admire Sticks' ability to make them laugh in all the right places. As soon as he was finished, Roger muttered something about the cold and said, "It's not even six yet. What do we do till eight?"

"Could watch the fat ladies bowl," Sticks said. "At least the building'll be warm."

Then Al whispered, "Someone's coming."

As if an alarm had sounded, Roger pressed the can he had into Brian's hand and hissed, "The beer." Brian stared blankly back at Roger, his gentle haze resisting the older boy's urgent tone. Roger said sharply, "Get it out of sight, Brian. It might be the park patrol."

The last words registered. Brian turned quickly and dumped the three unopened cans and the two open cans into the grass behind the fence. Then he turned to see what was going on. He heard Al say, "Ah, it's only some kid."

They could barely see the silhouette of someone walking toward them, his strides long and fluid, a basketball tucked under his arm. The figure entered the picnic area and headed for the path Roger and Al had used earlier.

The first thing to come clearly into sight was the kid's bright white sneakers and the red stripes of his sweat socks. His facial features became more distinct.

"Look who's here," Roger said, just loud enough for the other three to hear. "All basketball players walk a little light-footed, if you ask me. Bunch of faggots."

Sticks snorted. "Jocks're too tight."

Slowly, a cat stalking, Al rose to a standing position, his eyes on the approaching shape. Brian moved next to Roger. The kid hadn't slowed any or even glanced in their direction; he seemed oblivious to their presence.

"All they do is dribble a stupid ball and throw it through a stupid hoop." Roger's voice had taken on a harder edge. "And they all think they're such hot shits."

6

Sticks began moving toward the solitary figure, pausing only long enough to look over his shoulder, smile, and say, "Let's have a little fun before the dance."

Detective Sergeant Robert Wheeler ignored the stop sign, glanced left to check for oncoming traffic, and heaved the brown Plymouth around the corner. Even without stopping, the engine began making that sputtering, gasping noise that was the prelude to a stall.

He shifted the transmission to neutral and, coasting down the empty back street, pumped the accelerator several times. A muffled pop of unburned gas exploded from the tailpipe and then the engine began to hum regularly.

"There are children around here!" a woman shouted. "You could have killed one, but what do you care?"

Wheeler looked around and saw a heavy-set woman with white hair pointing at him. "Yes, you," she said. Still pointing, she pulled the terrier she had by the leash and came directly toward the slowly moving car. "You didn't stop. You didn't even signal. I saw you, so don't act so innocent."

She was almost at the passenger door when Wheeler put the car into drive and pulled away from her.

"What are you afraid of?" the woman called after him. "You'd better learn to drive before you run somebody over!"

Wheeler went about half a block before checking his rearview. He saw the woman standing in the street, glaring after him, while her dog sniffed at a pile of leaves.

No matter what you do you can't win, Wheeler thought, turning a corner to put some houses between him and the woman. Even if he explained that he was a cop and that his engine stalled if he went too slowly around corners, she probably wouldn't understand. Or that he always checked carefully before running a stop sign. You can't win.

He cruised down a few more tree-lined streets, noting the even procession of modest frame houses. In one front yard, some kids were playing football. Over there a young woman struggled with groceries while a child tugged at the hem of her coat. For Wheeler it was a normal late afternoon in November.

He was about to pass through the small shopping area when he remembered the Italian bread. Gail was making stuffed ziti with meatballs and she wanted a large loaf of hard, crunchy Tuscan pan bread that D'Andrea's bakery made.

Wheeler pulled the car into a space and was about to turn off the engine when the call box under the dashboard squawked incomprehensibly. He frowned and whacked the box with the side of his fist a few times. All that came out was a screechy static and the last words of the dispatcher's sentence: ". . . 546 Wilmont Road. Over."

Wheeler took the microphone. "Marge. This is Bob." He paused, waiting for a hum in the speaker to subside. "Could you run that by me again? I've got feedback."

"Sure thing," she said. She told him about the reported theft of two trays of prize-winning zinnias from Mrs. Florence White-Perkins' greenhouse. "She thinks it might have been neighborhood kids but she's not sure. She's not even sure when they were taken."

"Okay. I'll go by and see what happened," Wheeler said. "Then I'll probably be in for the day."

"Okay, Bob," the dispatcher said, adding, "you be real careful on this one, you hear."

"I always get my plant."

He pulled away from the shopping area and headed for Wilmont, all the while charting his moves for the next thirty minutes. He'd check out Mrs. Florence White-Perkins' story, then do a quick check of the streets surrounding Wilmont. Somewhere in his head he recalled that the street backing Wilmont was a dead end that stopped at an empty lot. If kids had taken the plants, that's probably where he'd find them, or what was left of them.

He sighed loudly, thinking that his day was becoming as predictable as the Plymouth's stalling or the white hairs he kept finding in his mustache and sideburns. He almost wished he were back in New York City. He'd had more interesting cases, and more of them, in his four years there than in seven here. Cases you could get so wrapped up in your mind became a computer loaded with facts and faces, your dreams a time when you sifted through details, hoping to unearth a new aspect so far overlooked.

No, things in Edgewater were definitely different. More peaceful and routine. Of course, that was why he'd left the city and come here in the first place.

Brian remembered seeing the boy's face in the school paper, the sports section most likely. It was the long jaw and the dark, thick eyebrows that stuck with him. The eyebrows especially. They ran in a straight bar, broken only briefly in the center, and gave the kid a permanently brooding expression.

Sticks maneuvered silently around the birches while Roger and Al glided in a path that would intercept the boy. Brian trailed Roger, hanging back a few paces and wondering what his part would be.

The boy saw Sticks, a darting shadow a little behind and to his right, but too late. With amazing agility, Sticks jabbed his fist into the basketball and sent it skidding along the ground toward Roger. Even in the dark, Brian could see that Sticks was slightly taller than the boy but not as solidly built.

"Hey, what the hell?" the boy asked, puzzled. He wheeled to face the attacking shadow, but Sticks dodged around another tree and skittered away in a wide semicircle. By the time the boy had whirled in a complete turn and located the ball, Roger was holding it in the air like a prize.

"Want to play ball?" he asked. "Hmmmm?"

"I've got to get going . . ."

"Aw, he's got to get home to Mama," Roger said. "You hear that?"

"Sweet Mama," Sticks shouted. "Toss that ball over here."

The boy took a few steps toward Roger. "Just give me the ball," he demanded. He held out his hand.

Roger lofted a long throw over the boy's head and right to Sticks, who caught it and immediately began dribbling the ball.

"Get a load of this ball handling," Sticks called out. He turned on his heels several times, passing the ball between his legs during each revolution. "The world's skinniest basketball player."

"And ugliest," Al shouted as he moved closer to Sticks. "I can't tell where the trees stop and you begin."

"Pure jealousy," Sticks said. "Now watch this one. Over the shoulder, a twirl and all without losing the beat."

While Sticks chattered away, Brian began moving away from Roger along an imaginary curving line that everyone, except the boy in the middle, seemed to be on. The boy stood, unmoving, fists clenched, watching Sticks' act. The game was obvious, and he seemed content to wait for it to play itself out.

Brian was equidistant from those on either side, right behind the boy, when Sticks tossed the ball to him.

Brian caught it easily and bounced it twice without much skill. The boy had had to turn to follow the ball's flight, and now he stared at Brian with a mixture of impatient anger and contempt that made Brian feel childish, guilty. Brian passed the ball to Roger.

Back and forth the ball sailed between Roger and Sticks, Sticks and Brian. Twice it zoomed over the boy's head, once only a foot or so above it. The boy kept his eyes on the ball but made no attempt to catch it. Al got the ball and threw it to Brian.

It was to Brian's left, and he had to move quickly if he wanted to intercept it. He stretched for it but misjudged its speed in the darkness, and his hands closed on air. The ball hit him in the chest and rolled directly toward the boy.

The boy only had to move a few steps to head the ball off, not hurrying and only leaning over when it was close. At the moment the basketball touched his hands, Sticks came sprinting up.

Brian saw the two boys collide, their arms and legs merging so he couldn't tell whose they were. The next instant, the ball was in flight again and Sticks whooped in triumph.

"You asshole," the boy snarled. He grabbed Sticks by the jacket and pushed him so hard that Sticks bounced off a tree and fell down.

"Hey, settle down," Sticks said, holding his hands up in case the boy took a swing at him. "We're just fooling around. No harm done."

"Yeah, well, I'm tired of this crap."

"Sure. Sure. Me, too."

"Did you hear?" Roger said, taunting. "The big man is tired and wants to go home. Don't you?"

The boy faced Roger. "Bastards."

"Don't get yourself all worked up," Roger said. He held the ball up in his palm. "Here. This is getting boring."

The boy walked across the open space to Roger.

"What are you trying to prove, anyway?" he asked.

"Nothing," Roger said evenly. "Nothing at all."

Roger remained motionless, a statue holding an orb, until the boy was a few steps away. Then in a single, swift motion that was a blur to Brian, Roger cocked back his arm as if he were going to send the ball on another looping journey. Instinctively, the boy reached into the air to block the throw, and as he did, Roger slammed the ball into the side of his face. There was a sickening thud of rubber against flesh and a muffled cry from the boy before he toppled over backward.

"Big basketball player," Roger said. "Can't even catch."

The boy rolled onto his side slowly and tried to push himself up, each movement deliberate and painful. His arms strained and his body began to rise. He was about halfway up when he faltered, his arms gave way under the weight, and he collapsed face down on the ground.

"I think you kayoed him," Al said, sauntering up to the sprawled-out figure. "A unanimous decision."

"Why'd you do that?" Sticks asked when he got to Roger.

"I didn't *do* anything. I was going to toss it to you and he jumped into the throw."

The boy began to move again. At first it was an imperceptible twitch of his head, slight and tentative, like the wing flutter a bird makes when alarmed. A few seconds passed and his head began to shake more rhythmically. Brian drew close. He could see the boy's right arm and leg also twitching in the same ceaseless pattern.

"What's the matter?" Sticks asked the boy, bending and nudging his shoulder. "Hey, can you hear me or anything?"

"Roll him over," Roger suggested.

Sticks rolled the boy so he was face up. Instead of the slight movement of before, his head jerked from side to side, eyes shut but mouth wide open, sucking in air noisily. The twitching stopped suddenly, but immediately his body contorted grotesquely, one leg bending and flopping to the side while his left hand reached straight out as if to grab something or someone. The boy's back arched and stiffened and a wet, gurgling sound escaped from deep in his throat.

"Jesus," Sticks murmured, standing away from the body and looking around at the others.

"Weird," Al said in a breathless whisper.

"Should we get help?" Brian asked. He looked to Roger, but the older boy was mute.

The boy's bent leg kicked out violently and hit Al in the shin, nearly sending him to the ground. Then the thrashing movement began again, this time more insistently. A tiny trickle of blood escaped the boy's nostril and began snaking down his cheek.

"Holy shit," Al said breathlessly. "Let's move it."

Roger backed away from the boy. Al turned abruptly and began running for the path. Roger was right behind him.

Sticks grabbed Brian's arm and dragged him away from the convulsing body. "Come on, Halihan. Move it!"

In the next instant, Brian was over the rail fence and running as hard as the others through the trees. Tall grass slapped at his jeans legs; sticker bushes reached out and tore at his hands and face.

They ran about two hundred feet when Al veered off the path and down a small incline. Brian could see Al's raincoat stretched out behind him, flapping crazily. Roger and Sticks followed.

"Hurry, Brian," Roger called without stopping.

Brian noticed that they were heading for a wall at the northern boundary of the park. The running jarred his vision, blurring it, though the shapes beyond the wall suggested a factory complex. Just before he cut off the path too, Brian came to a full stop and glanced around. Nothing in the picnic area stood out. Everything had been swallowed by the black.

He was down the incline a second later, his arms flailing wildly and his lungs drawing in gulps of air.

Ahead, Al leaped onto an oil drum and hoisted himself up the wall. Brian was close enough to hear Al's grunts as he struggled to pull his chubby body over the top and the slap when his feet landed on the other side. Roger jumped onto the barrel as Al had, but he stopped with only one leg over the wall, waiting for the others.

Sticks was next, barely hesitating as he vaulted and grabbed the top of the wall. With help from Roger, Sticks tossed himself over the wall.

Brian slowed as he approached the wall, no longer trusting his eyes in the dark. He judged the barrel's height correctly, but the lost speed threw his timing off. He made it onto the barrel, but the top of the wall was just beyond his reach.

"Here, take my hand," Roger said from the top.

"What about the blood?" Brian tried to look back again to where they'd left the boy.

"Don't worry about him, Brian. Just take hold."

A strong hand gripped Brian's wrist, and he felt himself lifted into the air. His free hand clawed for the top of the wall, grabbed for it and missed, grabbed again, and held. Brian pulled his head and torso over the top and then he heaved a leg over to secure his position.

"Thanks," he gasped. He stared down into the darkened courtyard.

"Brace yourself," Roger said, positioning himself to drop from the wall. "It's a long way down."

2

Wheeler had just speared another meatball with his fork when the telephone rang.

"Probably for me," Susan said, dropping her fork and pushing away from the table.

"Susan, chew your . . ." Gail's words were lost as her daughter hurried from the kitchen.

"Maybe she should take up track," Wheeler said, smiling.

Susan was back a second later. "It's for you, Dad. Someone from the station."

Wheeler's eyebrows rose in mild curiosity. He glanced at the kitchen clock, saw that it was just past seven, and mentally reassembled the duty roster. Hobart was on until ten, with Conte on call. Even if both were tied up, a uniformed cop could handle most ordinary cases.

"Did they say what it was about?" Gail asked.

"No," Susan said. "But it sounded official. They asked for 'Detective Sergeant Wheeler.'"

"Oh, well," Wheeler said in a drawn-out, accepting tone. "It's always something." He left the room, wiping his mustache carefully.

"I wonder what's up," Susan said.

"I wonder, too. And the next time the phone rings during dinner . . ."

"Okay, okay, Mom. I know what you're going to say. I just thought it might be Randy."

Wheeler came back into the kitchen. "Well, I've got to go out for a while. A problem at Van Bedford."

15

"Can't it wait, Bob?" Gail asked. "You hardly had a chance to touch your food."

" 'Fraid not. Hobart's at the Municipal Garage with a vandalism case and apparently Conte's sick. She's been feeling punk for a couple of days, and I guess it finally got the best of her. That leaves me."

"Ever-reliable you," Gail mumbled.

Wheeler stopped briefly at his plate and popped the meatball on his fork into his mouth. "Mmmmm. Best meatballs ever," he said, savoring the spices. "I better change into something warmer. Do you know where my boots are?"

"The utility room. I waterproofed them yesterday. And your flannel shirt's in the closet," Gail said as Wheeler left the room again. For an instant she felt as if she were constantly talking to the backs of her family. So Wheeler could hear in the other room, she spoke louder. "Your jeans are hanging up, too. I didn't have a chance to do the cords."

"I'm sorry about this. Really I am." He could sense Gail's displeasure.

"I know, it comes with the job," Gail said, getting up and taking her husband's plate from the table. "I was just hoping we could all be together for once on a Friday night."

"It's important tonight," Wheeler said, reappearing at the door and tucking his shirt into his jeans. "They found a body in the park."

"Oh," Gail said softly. "That's awful."

"Who was it?" Susan asked, her eyes widening. "Was it murder?"

"Susan, please," Gail said. She shuddered visibly. "Don't be so ghoulish."

"I was just wondering, that's all."

"It probably isn't so dramatic, so don't get your hopes up." Wheeler smiled at his daughter and kissed the top of her head.

"Do they know who it is?" Gail asked.

"No identity yet," Wheeler answered. "The call to the station

came from the park patrol and things are still a little confused."
He planted a quick kiss on Gail's cheek. "Might take a few hours
to get it straightened out."

"Okay, I'll keep the sauce warm." Gail wiped her hands on a
dish towel and lowered herself into her seat. "Do you have
everything?"

Wheeler went to the closet and put on his ski parka. Then he
reached up to the top shelf, took down his revolver, and clipped
it onto his belt in the back.

"I'm off," he called from the door.

"Take care, dear."

"I'm going to call Angela," Susan said. "She lives near the
park."

"Susan, please swallow your food first. . . ."

A fog, sharp with the first real chill of November, had eased
itself in from the river, its opaque fingers reaching up and cloud-
ing the streets. The added moisture didn't help the Plymouth's
disposition much, the engine bucking and coughing all during the
drive to the park.

Wheeler was halfway across the park's playing field when he
spotted a flashing red emergency light. He headed for the beacon
and brought the car to a halt when he drew even with a series of
probing headlight beams.

As he climbed over a rail fence, the shapes of the ambulance
and the park patrol's square little jeep, only vague lumps before,
took on recognizable form. Next, the lime green paneling of a
town police car jumped through the soupy fog. A radio crackled
and Wheeler saw figures moving between the vehicles.

He couldn't remember how many repetitions of this scene
he'd been a part of while at the 19th in New York. Scores of
them each year, especially during the long summers. And yet
he'd never been able to shake the feeling that settled on him as
he approached, knowing there was a body waiting for him. It
wasn't fear or nausea—you overcame that in time. It was more
embarrassment. Dying should be something private, to be ob-

served quietly—not announced with flashing lights and the inevitable procession of doctors, cops, and reporters who picked over everything for details to fill out their reports.

"Sergeant Wheeler," said a short, frail man whom Wheeler recognized immediately. The man came out of the circle of vehicles to greet Wheeler, blew some warmth into his cupped hands, and extended one. "I'm Jay Fry. Uh, park patrol."

"Hi," Wheeler said, somewhat perplexed. He'd worked with Fry less than twenty days before when the park's storage shed had been broken into. Well, he thought, coming across a body in the fog was bound to make most people a little formal. "What do we have?" he asked.

"A kid." Fry gestured without moving toward the jeep. A rumpled blue cloth, tiny from this angle, lay in the jeep's headlight beam. "He's seventeen. Name's . . . uh"—Fry pulled a torn piece of paper from his pocket and tilted it to catch some light—"William Janowski."

"Did you find him?" They went toward the body, Wheeler leading the way.

"No," Fry said. "A man walking his dog did. He's with the paramedics now. Do you want to talk to him?"

"That's okay. I'll talk with him later." Wheeler stood beside the cloth, delaying. This close, he could see the unmistakable shape of the body. He crouched down and gently slid the sheet away from the face.

The pasty whiteness registered first, luminescent and cold. Despite the shadows cast by the headlights, the facial features came next—the dark eyebrows; the long, strong jaw; and the mouth, slightly parted and strangely peaceful. It was the face of someone sleeping.

"How old did you say he was?" Wheeler touched the boy's neck with the back of his hand but found no trace of warmth.

"Seventeen. He looks older, doesn't he? He had this around his neck." Fry held up a shiny metal object on a chain. "MedicAlert tag. His name and birth date are on it." He handed the tag to Wheeler, who looked at it as Fry spoke. "He was an epileptic. The paramedics think he had a seizure and then a heart attack on top of it. Or a brain hemorrhage. They're not positive, of course. . . ."

Wheeler slipped the tag into his pocket and then pulled the sheet entirely away from the body. The right side reinforced the sleeping image, arm straight down at his side, leg stretched out. It was the left side that revealed something of the boy's last seconds alive, in particular the way the extended hand seemed to be clawing for a hold. "Is this the way he was found?"

"I'm not exactly sure. I really didn't notice. The paramedics tried to revive him, so I guess he must have been moved a little."

Wheeler took out his notepad and began jotting down the details Fry could recall: time of the initial discovery, when Fry and his partner had arrived, when the ambulance had come on the scene. He wanted to establish a precise sequence of events.

"Do you think the man could talk to me now?"

"He's in pretty rough shape," a uniformed patrolman said, joining them. "He's in his late sixties and had to do a lot of running to get help."

"And his dog ran off in all the commotion," Fry interjected. "My partner's out looking for the dog now."

"Is he going to be okay?" Wheeler asked. The patrolman was new on the force, short and burly, but while Wheeler could remember seeing him before, he couldn't recall his name.

"I think so. But it might be better to wait a while longer."

"Wouldn't want to rattle him any more," Wheeler said. "Your name's Kellogg, isn't it?" Kellogg nodded and Wheeler asked, "Could you shine your light down here?"

Kellogg snapped on his flashlight and swept it across the dead boy's face, erasing the shadows.

"Blood," Fry said in a kind of surprised gasp.

Wheeler grunted his agreement, wondering how Fry could have missed seeing the blood before. The feeble line of dark maroon, already dry and flaking in spots, began at the corners of the boy's nose and mouth and followed the natural valleys of the cheek, chin, and neck.

"Give me more light here," Wheeler said, indicating an area on the right side of the face just below the eye. Kellogg moved his light nearer and Wheeler leaned in for a better look. "See where the face is reddish? Looks like a pattern of some kind." Kellogg bent over closer. Fry stood away, glancing nervously toward the ambulance.

"Could be he hit a tree root when he fell," Fry offered. "That might be where the blood came from, too."

"I don't know. The pattern seems too regular for that," Wheeler said. He put his notepad on the ground and took the flashlight from Kellogg. "And there're no scrapes or cuts on the face or forehead. No dirt or grass stains either. As if he fell backward." He moved the light to within inches of the cheek. "See the swirling pattern?"

"Yeah," Kellogg said. "Does it mean anything?"

Wheeler shrugged. "Not necessarily. Did you find anything around here?"

"Just the boy's basketball. It's in the car." Kellogg trotted off toward his patrol car and returned moments later carrying the ball. Wheeler took the ball, shining the light on its textured surface. He slid the light to the boy's face and then back to the ball.

"Maybe he landed on the ball when he came down," Kellogg suggested tentatively.

"Possibly." Wheeler put the ball on the ground and handed the flashlight back to the patrolman. "Can't hurt to mention it in the report. Did you look around for anything else?"

"Gee, no," Kellogg said. "Sorry. I didn't see anything odd when I drove up so I didn't think to look."

"Okay, why don't we take a fast look around now." Wheeler pulled the cover back over the boy. A corner of the sheet buckled into an uneven series of waves, and he smoothed them out before standing.

20

"Maybe I should go find my partner," Fry said. "He's been gone a long time."

"I could use you here, Jay. It shouldn't take long." Fry seemed unsure but didn't leave. To make things easier for him, Wheeler told Fry to check the ground where the cars were parked, hoping the headlights and other people would calm him. He and Kellogg would check out the rail fence beyond.

"Are we looking for anything special?" Fry asked.

"No," Wheeler answered. "I just want to figure out exactly what happened here. Footprints would help. A crumpled cigarette pack. Anything unusual."

"Okay," Fry said, stumbling off to get his flashlight.

"Think he'll be all right?" Kellogg asked, looking after the vanishing guard.

"Let me tell you, I know how he feels. This fog goes right through you."

The two separated then, leaving the friendly circle created by the vehicles and lights, Kellogg heading straight to his designated section by the fence, Wheeler hustling to his car for his flashlight. On his way back, he let his light play over the ground assigned to Fry, just in case the man was too disoriented to spot anything. He saw nothing, so he angled toward the fence.

Once there, he began walking slowly along it, inching really, his beam glued to the ground. He saw a candy wrapper, soggy and torn and obviously very old. Scraps of rumpled paper hovered near the fence, clinging to the tall grass on the other side. Each close inspection told him these bits of debris had been there a long time. He continued.

About forty or fifty feet farther along, he came to a path that ran through the tall grass to, Wheeler supposed, a corner of the park near the factories. The path was worn by the passage of hundreds of feet, trampled hard and flat. He climbed over the fence and began scanning the ground and surrounding terrain.

He didn't feel when the fog turned to a heavy mist, the minutes rolled by so rapidly and he was concentrating so hard. He didn't even hear when Kellogg called out. At last Kellogg's shouts reached him, and he saw the young cop waving for him to come over.

Wheeler loped back along the path and hurried to Kellogg. When he got there, the other man was peering over the fence into the grass. Wheeler looked and saw three cans of beer attached to their plastic carrying strip with two opened cans leaning against these.

"Looks like somebody left in a hurry," Wheeler said, patting Kellogg's shoulder.

"I went right by them once," the young patrolman said, smiling and obviously excited with his find.

Fry came over to see what the commotion was about. "Anything here?" he asked.

"Kellogg found these."

"The park's always full of beer cans," Fry said. "Kids drink in here all the time."

"Do they leave unopened cans behind?" Wheeler asked, a little annoyed at Fry. He put his flashlight down and carefully sketched an overview of the area in his pad, marking the relationship of the body to the beer cans. He wrote down the brand name and size and even drew a rough picture of the orange price sticker that was plastered on the top of one of the cans. When he finished, he said, "I've got some rope in my car. I want to tie off the area around the body and over to here. Tomorrow, when it's light, we'll get some people in there"—he nodded toward the tangled woods—"to see if there's anything else interesting. It's too dark now."

"Can I go find my partner?" Fry asked.

"Sure," Wheeler said. To Kellogg he said, "I'll be needing your help. I still have to talk with the man who found the boy and to the paramedics. And I want to get some photos before we move the body. I'd appreciate it if you'd bag all these cans and the basketball and run them over to the forensic lab at Wellington."

"Fine," Kellogg said and then asked, "Violence?"

"Could be." Wheeler looked at the beer cans. "You'll need a piece of plastic and a rubber band for the open ones."

The patrolman nodded and trotted over to his car. Standing alone, Wheeler felt the icy sting of the mist. Five degrees colder and it'd be snowing, he thought. Far off, on the other side of the park, barking erupted and Wheeler wondered if the man's dog had been cornered.

As soon as Brian's feet hit the hard ground, Roger began dragging him along, pulling at his elbow until his feet started moving. He shook his head clear and finally started to pick up speed as the boys raced across the dark open court and then down a narrow alley.

Al was still in front, with Sticks right behind. Once Brian got his legs into gear, Roger let go and sprinted ahead. Brian felt the distance widening between him and the others and pumped his arms harder.

They went around a corner and the dirt turned to a rough, uneven skin of concrete. A row of garages faced one another across the driveway, each closed tight, their doors locked, windows blackened. Up ahead, Brian heard the quick chatter of feet trying to decelerate and Al disappeared between two buildings.

"Here. In here," Al shouted. "Hurry it up."

Sticks and Roger entered the shoulder-width space, with Brian just a step behind. Rusty hinges screeched and wood scraped along the ground. Al had yanked open the squat door of a storage shack and was motioning frantically to the others. "Inside. Quick," he said, waving his arms to get their attention. "Duck your head, Sticks." After Brian was inside, Al pulled the door shut behind him. Absolute blackness surrounded the four boys.

Brian stood still, trying to calm his wildly pumping heart. Someone, Al most likely, brushed past him and went to the back of the tiny building. Brian couldn't see very well, just shapes that meant nothing to him, and only knew where the others were by their irregular gaspings.

"I never thought . . . make it . . ." Sticks' words dissolved into a chaotic, exhausted jumble. "Outta shape, I guess," he barely managed to say. He moaned dramatically, and when he leaned over to open his wind passage, a shelf of empty oilcans crashed to the floor.

"Nothing like a graceful retreat," Roger said.

Al began laughing softly, tried to stifle it, failed, and laughed a little louder. Brian and Roger seemed to catch Al's mood and they began laughing too.

"Man's a real Fred Astaire," Al said.

"Hey, I'm dying over here," Sticks said. "Have some respect." He stumbled against the cans on the floor and the laughter continued, a nervous release of coiled tension.

"Never thought I'd see Al's legs move so fast," Sticks went on. "You really motored out there."

"Did you see me go over that wall?" Al asked, taking particular delight in the attention focused on him. "I should be in army training films."

"More like disaster movies," Roger said. He expelled a long stream of air from his lungs. "That really was a workout. My lungs feel like they're falling apart."

"How come you didn't move in the park, Brian?" Sticks asked. "I thought we'd have to crane you out of there."

"Aww, Brian did okay," Roger said before Brian could answer. He jabbed Brian in the ribs playfully. "Once he got going, he really smoked the trail. Right, Brian?"

"Yeah. I guess."

"He guesses," Sticks said. "You were hypnotized. Or drunk."

"Hey, lighten up," Roger grumbled. "Brian did just fine. Just fine." He shook himself. "Cold in here. Anybody have a cigarette?"

Al's raincoat rustled as he searched for a pack. A white cylinder floated across the air and a moment later a match flared and

24

illuminated Roger's face. Beads of sweat glistened on his forehead, and when Brian felt his own, he found it moist, too.

Al said, "You really leveled that guy. Pow and he was out for the count."

"Yeah; how come you hit him?" Sticks asked.

Roger inhaled deeply and passed the cigarette to Al. "I told you, he jumped into the throw. And I thought he was going to punch me. I just happened to beat him to it."

"I wonder if he knows what hit'm? Or who?" Sticks put his hands in his pockets and began jiggling coins idly. "You know who that was, don't you? Janowski. I didn't recognize him until he dumped me on the ground."

"The basketball player," Roger explained to Brian.

"Now he'll probably get some of his goon buddies to stuff me into a locker or something."

"You worry too much, Sticks," Roger said. "I could barely see him, so I'll bet he didn't get a good look at any of us either. Too dark and too much going on."

Brian recalled the penetrating stare Janowski had fixed on him when he had the ball. If Brian could make out his features in the dark, then Janowski could see him too. . . . The cigarette came to Brian, interrupting his thoughts, and he inhaled deeply to distract himself, the smoke filling his mouth and tickling his throat. He coughed but covered it by asking, "Think he's okay?"

"Yeah, I wonder what all that shaking and stuff was about," Sticks added quickly. "He didn't look so hot when we left him."

"I just grazed his jaw and he blacked out. That's all." A touch of anger crept into Roger's face. "I mean, forget it. If it makes you all feel better, I'll take the blame if anything happens. Okay? Happy?"

"I just want to avoid trouble," Sticks said. "That's all, Roger. No one wants to lay it all on you."

"Sounded that way."

"If anything does happen," Al said, "I'm going to say Janowski took the first swing. Who can prove different?"

"Nobody," Brian answered. It was possible, he told himself. Janowski had moved toward Roger; he might have been aiming a punch at him.

"It's our word against his," Sticks sighed. "I just hope it never comes to that."

They all talked awhile about what had happened, how Janowski had come at Roger, and how they'd all panicked and run off like a bunch of scared kids fleeing a ghost when the kid fainted. Sticks even managed to do an imitation of Janowski's shaking fit, complete with flailing arms and rolling head. Inevitably, however, the conversation always steered itself around to how they'd handle Janowski in the future.

Roger said, "I honestly don't think he recognized any of us, but he might prowl around looking for four kids. It might be smart to forget the dance and stay low for a few days."

"Real cops-and-robbers stuff," Sticks said.

"Right," Roger said. "I don't have any classes with him, so I won't run across him much in school. It'd be good to keep quiet about this, don't tell anybody."

"Think we should go back?" Brian asked.

"Believe me, Brian. He's okay." Roger moved to the door and peeked out. "We're better off if we just get out of here and let it all die down."

"Okay."

"Good. Why don't you check outside, Al. Then we can get moving."

Al crossed the shack and slipped out the door as quietly as possible. The others remained silent and anxious, waiting. At last, Brian coughed just to make some noise.

"Think he fell into a hole?" Roger asked.

It was quite a while before the door opened and Al swung back inside.

"Where were you?" Sticks wanted to know.

26

"Went back to the wall," Al answered. "Everything's clear. I checked up the driveway a little, too. There's a night watchman around somewhere. I saw his hut."

"Did you see him—Janowski—when you went back?" Sticks asked.

"I'm only five six. I'm not about to go looking for that gorilla."

"He just runs from them." Roger held the door open and said to Al, "You have a pretty good fix on the place. Why don't you take Sticks out first. Brian and I will follow."

The door opened and Al and Sticks left. Roger watched them go up the narrow passage and turn left toward the street. Before he came back inside, he tossed the cigarette against the opposite wall, creating an explosion of orange yellow sparks.

"Thanks for sticking by me."

"That's okay. I mean, everybody did." Still, Brian was pleased by the compliment.

"I wonder about Sticks. He's okay and all, but sometimes he . . . you know, bails out when things get hairy. Come on, let's get out of here."

They went to the driveway and followed it toward River Road. Wisps of fog seeped in around the factory buildings, probing the shadows and curling up the drainpipes. Brian hadn't noticed the fog earlier.

Roger said, "Sometimes when we're just crapping around, Sticks'll start getting jumpy. All fidgety like an old lady. Then he has those quiet spells. It's hard to figure out what's going on in his head."

There was a long, hacking, wet cough to their right, far off and somewhere they couldn't see.

"Night watchman," Roger whispered. They came to a gap between buildings and paused. "There." Roger pointed to the watchman's hut. A yellow light beamed from the three windows facing the driveway; gray black smoke oozed from the tall stovepipe. They could see the top of the watchman's balding head, bent forward and immobile, as if he were napping or watching television. He wouldn't leave his warm shelter unless a bomb went off.

"He's okay," Roger said, after they'd crept across the gap safely and put some distance between them and the hut. "Janowski. He was trying to get up when I went over the wall."

"Really?" Brian felt relieved. "I tried to look back but it was too dark."

"From the wall you could see. He might come out of it with a black eye and a headache but not much else." They came to the main road and paused at the crumbling curb. No cars moved in the fog and already Al and Sticks were gone. "I wish I had my car to give you a ride," Roger said apologetically. "Well, I'll talk to you at school."

"Sure," Brian said.

"And thanks again."

Then Roger crossed the street, his body flaring into detail when he walked under a street light. He shoved his hands into his pockets and faded into the night.

When the sound of Roger's steps disappeared, Brian turned and looked back down the driveway, debating. The fog was thick, wall to wall, and Roger had said that he'd seen Janowski moving. He'd be taking a needless chance by going back. He stepped off the curb and headed home.

A block or so later, he cut through a yard that led to Rose Street. It was a slightly longer route, since Rose twisted and turned in a couple of places, but it was quieter here. Fewer people lived on the street and drivers stayed clear because of the deep potholes that scarred the blacktop.

Brian found himself curiously ebullient, satisfied. He envisioned himself as part of a commando group that had just pulled off a difficult mission. It was an image that pleased him. He didn't like the fact that Janowski had been decked—even so, it made him feel more a part of the group, closer to them and bound by the action. The friends he'd had before were okay and he'd been close to them until this year. It was only since summer that he'd begun to see them as young, less independent, and less adventuresome.

He marveled at how quickly things had changed for him this year. He started school off by meeting Amy and they'd been going out ever since. Then, less than three weeks later, he'd met Roger and they'd hit it off pretty well. Surprisingly well, considering that Roger had two years on Brian. Everything seemed to be coming together for him.

It wasn't until he actually saw his house that he thought of his mother. She'd see him and know instantly that he'd been hacking around. Her Italian radar, his father called it. Brian saw it as a reflex; she suspected the worst at all moments.

He pulled a handkerchief from his pocket and wiped the sweat and facial oils off. Next he ran his comb through his hair. Try to act natural, he told himself.

At the back door he paused and looked inside. He could see his mother clearing the table of serving dishes and plates, scraping them and piling them in an already overloaded sink. She was short, five feet tall at best, and plump, and despite an eternally weary look in her eyes, possessed with energy to spare. He couldn't see his father or his little sister Patti, and he guessed that dinner had just ended. He decided to plunge in.

"Hey, Mom," he said, pushing the door open. "What's cooking?"

"Dinner's over. I thought you were going to get a hamburger with your friends."

"Changed our minds." He picked up a cold green bean and nibbled at it. "And I wouldn't miss your world-famous meat loaf for anything."

"Don't throw that bull around here. You and your friends ran out of mischief to do, so you came home. Right?"

"Sorta." He looked away from her.

"And now you expect me to do another meal just for you. Right?" He didn't answer. "Well, do you?"

"A sandwich maybe. I'll make it myself."

"Never mind that. Just remember next time this isn't a restaurant." He nodded sheepishly. "Sit down and I'll warm these things. I don't know about teenagers these days. Always running around. No schedules. One of these days you'll miss me. I'll die and there won't be anyone here to clean and iron and wash clothes. . . ."

She was in fine form. Talking away while whipping together his meal. When his plate was heaped with steaming food, she brought it over to him.

"Your father and Patti went to get some ice cream. If you hurry we can all have dessert together . . . if your schedule allows, of course."

"Give me a break," Brian said.

"I'll give you a break, Mr. Stayout. Right in your noodle." She smiled broadly and mussed up his hair like she did when he was small. "Are your hands clean?"

3

*T*he next morning Brian smelled the pancakes cooking all the way upstairs and knew his father had manned the stove. On his way down, he heard Patti ask, "When we eating?" and could imagine her wiggling around in her chair impatiently, holding her plate out.

"Now, honey," his father said, "perfection takes time, especially with my Halihan Specials." Brian got to the kitchen just as his father flicked the spatula and a pancake made nervous flips in the air before returning to the griddle. His father beamed proudly.

"I'm hungry," Patti announced, extending her plate.

"Okay. The Bottomless Pit gets the first batch." Brian's father was tall and angular with the quick, assured movements of an athlete. "Morning Brian."

"Mornin', everybody." Brian stretched and yawned.

After putting a load of pancakes on Patti's plate, his father turned to face Brian's mother, gently wagged the spatula in her direction, and said, "Jim thinks the investment is sound."

"I don't know," Brian's mother said, drawing out the words. "Everywhere I look it's inflation up, interest rates up, food prices up—and stocks down. And we have to think of the kids' futures. I don't know."

"Two or three pancakes, Brian?"

"A couple will be fine," Brian said, plopping himself into his chair. It always amazed Brian that his parents were such opposites. Not just physically, but also in the way they acted. No matter what happened, count on his mother to pick at it and worry. His father was more analytical about situations, taking his time to see the angles before making any judgments.

"Anyway," his father said, "this isn't stocks. It's real estate. And Jim thinks we'll be able to rent enough space to cover all our costs in the first year, year and a half." He said all this calmly, persuasively, in the tone Brian supposed he used to explain insurance plans to a client. His father's voice brightened. "So how are they, Empty Stomach?"

"My stomach's not empty anymore," Patti said, using her most revoltingly cute voice.

"But your head's empty," Brian said.

"Is not."

"Is too, Bubble Brain."

"Children!" Their mother looked up from the headlines and frowned at Brian, then went back to scanning the paper. Patti stuck her tongue out at Brian, shoveled some more pancakes into her mouth, and tried to look sweet.

"Here you go, Brian." A steaming plate of pancakes settled in front of Brian. His father said, "We could take half the money from savings and get the rest with a second mortgage. We could handle the payments comfortably."

"Still and all . . ." his mother said, shaking her head stubbornly. She looked at Brian. "Oh, Brian. Did you know the Janowski boy?"

"Huh?" He stopped buttering his pancakes. "No. I don't know him. Why?"

"It says here"—she flipped back through the pages until she came to the article she was looking for—"says he was from your school. A senior."

There was a tiny jolt in Brian's head, something almost physical that froze his thoughts and his body. The words "*was* from your school" echoed in his brain and a strange, lightheaded feeling overcame him.

"Can I have more, Daddy?" Patti asked. "They were real good."

"He was found dead last night. In Van Bedford Park." His mother didn't look away from the article but asked, "Is that the park over by the river? I always get that one confused with the one near the railroad."

"Yeah," Brian said, his throat dry. "I think it is, anyway." He looked down at his food and an odd, sweet-tasting fluid filled his mouth, the way it usually did just before he threw up.

"Such a shame," his mother was saying. "It says he was a star basketball player and had a number of scholarship offers from colleges." She clucked her tongue in a sad way. To Patti she said, "If you finished all your pancakes, you can have more."

"I did. Look." Patti held her plate up and tilted it so the excess syrup began to drip off.

"Here," Brian said, sending his plate across the table to Patti. "Why don't you take these?" His mother shot him an inquiring glance and he added, "I forgot I was supposed to call somebody early today. Slipped my mind. I'll be right back."

His sister grabbed the plate as he slid from the chair and the room.

"Strange," he heard his mother say. "His face looked odd. Flushed."

"Might be a touch of flu," his father said.

Brian vaulted up the stairs, taking three at a time, and was nearly running full out when he reached his room. He searched his dresser drawer frantically for the stray bits of paper that had telephone numbers on them. He found Roger's.

He went into the hall, grabbed the phone, and hauled it into his room, punching out Roger's number as he kicked the door closed. When Roger's mother answered, he asked for Roger as calmly as he could.

"Hey, Brian," Roger said casually. "What's up? I thought we were going to . . . well, you know."

"I know, but everything's changed. Everything. It's the kid. Janowski."

"I told you he wouldn't bother us. He doesn't . . ."

"He's dead, Roger." Saying it sent a chill through Brian; he lowered his voice. "My mother just read it in the paper."

"What?"

He wished he could be calmer, more controlled. His voice quivered noticeably when he said again, "He's dead. They found him in the park."

"Take it easy," Roger said, but even his composure was fading. "Maybe it was somebody else. A mistake."

"I don't think so, Roger."

"Okay, don't hit the panic button." The next words came out harshly. "Nothing goes right. Nothing." Then there was a long silence.

"Roger?"

"I'm thinking, Brian."

"We've got to do something."

"I know," Roger said absently. "I'll call the others and we'll have a meeting to talk things over. Say in about an hour near the tracks."

"What are we doing to do? He's . . ."

"I heard. Just be at the Plank Street bridge and we'll talk."

Before Brian could answer, the dial tone began buzzing in his ear.

As usual, the door to the detectives' office was jammed so Wheeler had to lean into it with his shoulder as he turned the knob. Inside, Hobart sat at his desk, cradling a steaming cup of black coffee between his hands.

"It's going to snow soon. I can feel it in my fingertips." It was Hobart's way of greeting.

"It is colder today," Wheeler acknowledged, squeezing between his and Hobart's desks. The tiny office held three desks, with Hobart and Wheeler against the rear wall, their backs to a multipaned window. Conte's desk was on an inside wall, along with the filing cabinets and a coat rack nobody used. The space remaining was taken up by a pair of battered wooden chairs. Before sitting, Wheeler tossed his jacket onto one of the chairs.

"I thought you were going home right after the search," Hobart said.

"I was, but we didn't turn up anything. Kicked around in the grass from seven until a little while ago and all we got was wet feet. I was hoping that Wellington report would be here with something interesting." Wheeler searched through the heaps of paper on his desk. "Your friend Brooks said he'd have it here by ten."

"If Brooks said he'd have it for you, he will. Be patient." Hobart swiveled his chair so he faced Wheeler. He said, "You're really on this one, aren't you? I saw your preliminary report."

"Looked interesting, that's all. I wouldn't say I was 'on it,' though."

"I didn't mean anything by it," Hobart said. He raised his cup to his lips and sipped the hot liquid carefully, his eyes on the younger detective. "I thought the information looked interesting myself. Fact, if I was a normal chief of detectives, I'd muscle in and give you the Municipal Garage mess. No, it's definitely worth the time." He lowered the cup onto his ample beer gut and stared into it. "Must be rough, though. I have a son who's twenty-two and I can imagine what the parents are going through."

"The father especially," Wheeler said, recalling vividly the way the man had looked the night before, clinging to his wife's arm. "He blamed himself for letting his son act normal."

"That's the way it usually is," Hobart said thoughtfully. "Did you mention the facial marks to the parents?"

Wheeler shook his head. "The family doctor requested an autopsy, so I didn't think it was necessary. I filled him in—and the medical examiner."

"Good," Hobart said, taking another sip of coffee. "And if I remember correctly, the hospital usually has its reports released by noon. That'll tie up most of the loose ends for you." He snapped his fingers, as a slight frown made his lips pucker. "Oh, I almost forgot. Cummings saw the requisition for the lab work this morning and came huffing around about the $150 fee."

Wheeler wrinkled his face in disgust. "Anything in particular?"

"No, just the usual." The usual was Directive C-43, a precisely worded memo that limited lab work to obvious court cases and had already saved the town several thousand dollars.

"Cummings can go shove it." Wheeler pitched forward toward Hobart. His voice grew louder. "I mean, a kid, a seventeen-year-old kid died."

The older man held up his hands. "Hold it, Bob. Hold it. I told Cummings I had approved the fee. He just wanted to be sure procedure had been followed."

"Little bureaucrat."

"And I only mentioned it so you'll know in case he collars you in the hall. For both our sakes. You know the procedures stick in my throat too."

"Sorry, Andy." Wheeler looked at his pile of undone paperwork, half of which had become required since Cummings' arrival two years before. "I appreciate the warning."

The phone rang and Hobart grabbed it, snatching a pad at the same time to jot down information. He talked for a few minutes but only wrote down a name and address before hanging up.

"Man's dog is missing and he thinks it was dognapped for medical experiments over at the college." He blew a stream of air between his lips. "Sure you wouldn't want me to handle the Janowski case?"

"No way." Wheeler studied his pile of papers again and gave a bored sigh. "Look," he said. "I really don't feel like waiting for those lab reports. I think I'll check out the price sticker on the beer."

"Still your own time until noon."

"Know any stores that use these stickers?" Wheeler asked,

showing Hobart his hastily done sketch from the night before. There was nothing terribly distinctive about it except for the deep, v-shaped notches at each end and its orange color.

"I'm an expert on beer," Hobart said, patting his stomach. "Don't know anything about stickers." When Wheeler didn't respond but only stared at his sketch thoughtfully, Hobart added, "You might check by the factories. There are a lot of delis over there. Here"—he pulled a thin telephone directory from his desk—"this might be of some help."

"Thanks. I guess it is a long shot. Probably won't lead anywhere."

Wheeler slipped from behind his desk and grabbed his jacket, stuffing the directory into the pocket as he went to the door.

"I'll give Brooks a call to ask about the report." The door creaked shut and Hobart called out, "Oh, and see if you can pick up a get-well card for Conte."

While the Plymouth warmed up, Wheeler opened the directory to the liquor and spirits section; he counted ten stores. Next a mental picture of Edgewater's shape came to him. The town sprawled along five miles of the Iselton River but was flat and narrow, with a street grid designed to facilitate walking. Van Bedford Park was situated near the center of the town, with eight of the liquor stores located close by.

He eased the car from the parking lot and headed for Gaslight Wine and Spirits. Since no one remembered seeing a car in the Van Bedford parking lot, he assumed that whoever had left the beer had been on foot. He'd work away from the Gaslight, following the most-used streets.

Halfway over to the liquor store, he stopped to get the local newspaper and a card for Conte. The Janowski boy's picture was on the front page of the *Tribune*, with the simple headline *Local Youth Found Dead* above it. A glance at the opening paragraph told Wheeler the story would be the usual patchwork of fluff information—the boy's age and address, his school, his activities, and a list of surviving family members. Just enough to let readers know who had died and where without forcing them to become involved past the five minutes' reading time. The story wouldn't mention Mr. Janowski's trembling, colorless lips or the way his eyes looked to each person for help.

The Gaslight's owner didn't use the kind of stickers Wheeler described; the best he could do was say that, because of the deep perforations, the stickers were probably run off on an old machine. Wheeler headed down the street to Tinero's Liquors

He tried to recall the feeling he'd had the night before when he turned from where Kellogg had found the beer cans to where the boy was. The distance was so short that the connection seemed obvious. It wasn't, of course. The connection would have to be proved, not assumed; still, something in his head, something instinctual, told him he was on the right trail.

After an hour, Wheeler had amassed eight checkmarks in the directory, each signifying a strikeout, and a load of information on stickering machines.

He checked his watch. He still had forty-five minutes before it was time to relieve Hobart. If he hustled, he could cover two or three more stores. The rest would have to wait until later in the day when he got off. The feeling that he was running around trying to catch an elusive phantom entered his mind. Maybe one he'd created himself.

He pulled up to MacPheason's Delicatessen. He was on his own time now, so no one could gripe. Besides, you never knew what might turn up.

Brian quick-stepped across the Plank Street bridge, glancing furtively over his shoulder, checking and double-checking for the brown car. At the end of the bridge he slithered through an opening in the hedge and hurried down a rocky hill to the concrete base where the others were waiting.

He was panting loudly when he reached them. "They know," he said between gasps for air. "The cops. I saw one at Mac-Pheason's." He explained quickly how he'd gone by the deli and spotted the police emblem on a parked car's license plate. Inside the store a man, a detective, Brian assumed, was talking with the old man and gesturing toward the display case where Brian had gotten the beer.

"Maybe he was buying some bologna and beer," Al joked feebly.

"I knew something was going to happen," Sticks said, kicking at the hard ground. "I could feel it last night."

"I was just showing this to Al and Sticks." Roger handed Brian a copy of the *Tribune*, folded over several times so only one story was readable. A photo of Janowski smiled out at Brian. "See. Here at the bottom. It says he died of a brain hemorrhage caused by his seizure. Read it yourself."

"I still don't get the point," Sticks said. "We know he had a seizure."

"But it doesn't say anything about him being hit. For all we know, he might have gotten up and come after us—and then had another seizure. He might have gone back and played some more basketball, too. Who knows? The important thing is that there's nothing about him being hit."

"What about the cop Brian saw?" Sticks said. "Once they latch on to something, they don't let go. I can tell you that."

"Shouldn't we tell somebody what happened?" Brian asked. "I mean, we were there."

A silence overcame them, broken only by the whoosh of traffic going across the bridge. The metal girders rumbled and specks of flaking rust sprinkled down on the four boys standing below. Roger said, "Look, when Brian told me about Janowski, that he was dead . . . well, I went blank. I didn't know what to say or think. Or do. Right, Brian?"

Brian nodded.

"And I know I hit him. But I still don't think I hit him hard enough to . . ." He gestured to the paper Brian was holding. "But if we tell anybody, they won't believe us. They'll think the worst."

"I didn't know he was an epileptic," Al said almost solemnly. "Who'd've guessed, the way he was always playing basketball?"

"And we had to be there," Sticks grumbled. "He has an attack and we had to be there. Damn."

"What about the cop?" Brian asked. "The one I saw."

"Might have been a coincidence," Roger said. "Maybe he did find the beer and was checking to see who bought it. I don't know." He shrugged. "I'll tell you, though, if they find out we were there, it isn't going to look too good for us. Especially with Sticks' record."

At mention of his record, Sticks' face clouded over, a blend of anger and self-pity. "Some luck."

"I'll go along with whatever you guys decide," Roger said, his voice soft. "If you want to go in and tell the cops . . . it's up to you."

Brian stood quietly, hoping a freight train would go by or a factory whistle would blow—anything to give him some precious moments to think things through. All he heard was the impatient clicking of dry weeds on the hill below them.

He looked up to find Roger staring at him, waiting for his answer. Brian said, "We don't really have much choice, do we? They might think we beat him up or something."

"I really didn't hit him very hard," Roger added. "It was an accident, but I don't think many people will believe us."

"Maybe if we give it a few days, it'll all blow over," Al said. "Calm down, you know."

"All I know is that I can't afford any more trouble," Sticks said. "My parents don't want anything to do with me now. If they heard this . . . Jeez, I might as well pack my bags, for all the help they'd give me."

After this, Roger tried to reassure them all about the cop Brian had seen, even reading sections of the newspaper article out loud to them. "They'd have mentioned it if they thought something had happened to Janowski, believe me," he said, pacing in a

40

tight circle and gently slapping the paper into his palm. "And if something does happen, all we'll say is that we were in the park drinking beer and never saw Janowski. They can't prove otherwise."

"I hope you're right," was all that Sticks said.

Twenty minutes later, they split up. Sticks went down the hill to the railroad tracks and from there up to the North Bergan Street crossing. Roger, Al, and Brian climbed the dirt path to the street above.

"See what I mean about Sticks?" Roger said to Brian once they were through the hedge.

"I'm pretty jittery myself," Brian said.

"We all are," Roger went on. "But it's different with him. He's ready to go over the edge." The older boy made a face as if to say "It takes all kinds," then continued. "I guess we should keep an eye on him just in case."

"Yeah," Al agreed. "Just in case."

After saying good-bye, Roger and Al disappeared down the street away from Brian.

Ordinarily Brian would have liked to accompany them, be a part of whatever they might do. But today he only wanted to be alone for awhile, to let the day and weekend pass without taking part in it. Maybe things would calm down, as Al had said. He crossed the bridge, though his pace slowed when he thought of his mother and her questioning glances. He really didn't need that either. He could always go over to Amy's, of course. As inviting as that sounded, though, he was sure his moodiness would betray him. He chose to walk up block after block instead, killing time with each step.

A few blocks from the bridge, he was startled when a brown car slid up to the curb beside him and its horn blared. The vision of the detective flared before him; he froze, waiting to hear his name barked out harshly, to be seized by strong hands.

Instead, he heard a house door slam followed by the patter of footsteps on concrete. When he looked, he saw a young girl carrying a battered trombone go sprinting past him to the waiting car. A second later the car pulled away.

Brian could almost laugh at his reaction. He'd either been watching too many detective stories on TV or he'd caught some of Sticks' edginess. Then the sobering vision of the detective reappeared. . . . Brian jammed his hands into his jacket and, hunched against the chilly breeze, he continued wandering the streets.

4

"*B*ob?" Gail came out of their bedroom, her slippers flopping along the floor to the tiny utility room. "Bob, it's almost one-thirty."

Wheeler was bent over his desk, intently examining a photograph of the park, the image dark and murky but still revealing enough to give a good idea of the scene. He didn't notice Gail coming up next to him or her shadow as it fell across the photo.

"Bob?" she touched his shoulder and he looked up quickly.

"Oh, it's you. Didn't hear you." He dropped the photo on top of the rest of the Janowski file papers, adding, "There's got to be something here."

"Maybe you found everything there is to find. You said the medical report came in. . ."

"That," Wheeler said in a dismissive tone. The medical examiner had attributed the boy's death to a ruptured aneurysm of the basilar artery. The aneurysm had grown at the base of the brain, undetected by the boy's doctor in routine examinations and unnoticed by the boy, except for some dizziness and an occasional headache. The strenuous exercise the boy had had that afternoon, the increase in his blood pressure, had brought on a grand mal seizure—and the artery membrane had given way finally. At least that was the M.E.'s reconstruction of what might have happened.

As for the injuries to the right side of the face—the burst capillaries on the cheek, the three loose teeth, and the broken cartilage in his nose—the M.E. speculated that they had occurred after the seizure due to a fall. "Don't you see," Wheeler

43

said, "he's got these things backward. There were no abrasions, no cuts or scrapes on the face. No dirt. If he'd fallen on his face with enough force to cause a bruise, he'd have been marked somehow."

"Maybe the examiner didn't see it that way," Gail said, keeping her tone light but sympathetic.

"I don't see how he could have missed it."

"Well, he is a doctor and he's supposed to report what he finds."

"He's a bureaucrat at heart," Wheeler grumbled. "He only saw what he wanted to see."

Gail ignored the comment, knowing that once her husband had latched onto something, he didn't let go easily. She rubbed the sleep from her eyes and tried unsuccessfully to stifle a yawn. "I'm going to make some hot chocolate. Want some?"

"Hmmm?"

"Hot chocolate. Want some?"

"Oh. No, thanks." He shuffled through the case's papers once again while Gail padded off to the kitchen. He heard the sound of the refrigerator opening, milk being poured into a pot, the puff as she lit the gas burner. He said, "I'm not questioning the medical details, you understand. I can see how the seizure would lead to the burst artery. Gail?"

"I can hear you," she said, sticking her head out of the kitchen and motioning toward the room where Susan slept.

"Okay. Sorry," he said in a hoarse whisper. "It's not that stuff that burns me. It's the fact that he's so positive about how the facial injuries happened."

"He did say it was speculation in the report." Gail came out of the kitchen carrying her steaming cup. "You said he made that clear."

"But he didn't even suggest any other possibilities."

Worse still, the lab report from Wellington hadn't been of any real help. It had turned up three sets of fingerprints on the beer cans recovered at the scene, but none were the Janowski boy's.

44

There was nothing to directly tie in Janowski with whoever had been drinking the beer.

A scowl crossed Wheeler's face as he thought of the beer cans. The deli owner, MacPheason, had identified the orange stickers as his. "Been usin' them for almost twenty years," the old man had said. "No doubt about that." But he did have doubts about the beer being stolen. "I was here all day," he'd said. "Nobody could have gotten in and out of the store without me hearin'm."

There just weren't any openings—not from the M.E., the Wellington report, or MacPheason—to justify much more departmental time on the case. If only they'd been in Van Bedford on Friday night, Wheeler thought. They'd see the way it all fit together immediately.

"Sure you don't want some chocolate?" Gail asked. "The milk's still hot."

"No," he said. "I want to go over this material again."

"Why don't you come to bed? You'll see it clearer in the morning. You might even get an inspiration in a dream."

"Can't just now." Wheeler was far away again, trying to pull back that feeling, the electric jolt that came when he recollected Friday night's cold mist and the location of the beer cans near the body. If he could get close enough to it all again, he was sure it would give him a clear direction to follow. What he couldn't figure out was why no one else sensed what he did.

"Well, don't stay up too long," Gail said. She went over to him and kissed the top of his head. Then she flip-flopped back to their bedroom and left him alone.

Brian woke late on Sunday morning. He felt tired and stiff, as if he hadn't closed his eyes at all during the night.

At breakfast he picked at his scrambled eggs and pushed the sausage links around his plate, all the while ignoring Patti's jabber. He was used to tuning her out, but not to the pictures that flooded his mind when he did it that morning—a piece of film that began a second before Roger hit Janowski and followed the whiplash snap of the head, the boy's falling and convulsing.

At first the replaying of the ball smashing against Janowski's face had sickened Brian. He could recall the sound. Feel the impact. It was so real it made his stomach knot up.

He'd forced himself to see this moment again and again, hoping to discover exactly what had happened. Then the variations began. In one, the angle of Roger's throw was steep, as if he was just going to loft the ball over Janowski's head to Sticks. In another, Janowski rose up on his toes, actually left the ground, to block the throw. It could have happened that way, Brian told himself. It might have been a freak accident.

That's when Brian realized he'd lost it. He'd tried out so many variations, tried so hard to find one he could accept and live with, that he'd lost the original memory forever. The only truth he was left with was the thud of the ball against Janowski's face.

"Are you okay?" His mother reached across the table and placed her hand on his forehead. "You look odd."

"No," Brian said, shaking his head to dislodge his mother's hand. "I mean yes. I'm okay. I was just thinking about a history test I have tomorrow."

"You were flushed like a toilet," Patti said through a mouthful of half-chewed eggs.

"Oh, shut up," Brian snapped. "Little nerd."

She made a face at him.

"That's enough," their mother said. "It's Sunday and we don't need an argument. Patti, why don't you go wake your father up. It's almost time for church."

His sister made another face at Brian, then left the kitchen.

His mother asked, "Are you coming to church with us? There's going to be a new priest this week."

"I don't think so. I have to meet the guys in a little while. And there's all the studying I have to do, too."

"It's your decision." She didn't try to hide her disappoint-

46

ment. "Do you think you'll be home for dinner? We're eating at three."

"I'll try." Brian made an attempt to eat some of his breakfast.

"Make sure you bundle up," his mother said. "It's supposed to get colder later on. Did you have a sore throat?"

"Mom. Believe me. I'm all right."

It was his day off, but Wheeler found himself in the Plymouth heading for the Janowski house. The way the reports were stacked against him, it would be hard to wangle much time tomorrow, especially with Cummings always poking around.

He pulled onto Wexler Drive and discovered a block of narrow, three-story houses built closely together, each with a small patch of front yard. Quick glances to either side told Wheeler that the people here cared for their homes. Most were freshly painted or recently sided with aluminum, the walks and lawns and curb clear of the pesky brown leaves that haunted most other areas of the town.

He glided by number 29 Wexler and knew by the long line of cars that any chance of a solitary visit was out of the question. Eight houses down the street he found a space and pulled in, the tail of the Plymouth blocking access to a driveway. He flipped down the passenger-side sun visor so his police insignia showed clearly.

At the Janowski house, a small elderly woman with sharp brown eyes opened the door a crack to him. She looked at him quizzically.

"I'm Detective Wheeler," he announced. "I wonder if I might speak to Mr. or Mrs. Janowski."

"Oh," the woman chirped, a weak smile appearing on her lips. She swung the door open wide and Wheeler stepped in, the overly warm air and smell of food enveloping him. "You're the nice man who brought Helen and Michael to the hospital. They really appreciated your kindness, you know. Really."

"I don't want to interrupt the family," Wheeler said, looking over the woman's shoulder into the living room just off the hallway. He saw a dozen or so people clustered there, their voices soft and low, merging into a somber background murmur. A few looked up at him, curious. "It won't take more than a few minutes."

"Oh, that's okay. It might do them some good." The woman walked down the long, carpeted hall, Wheeler at her heels, and stopped at a closet. "I'm Helen's Aunt Janet," she said and at the same time took his coat.

"Nice to meet you."

"Helen's with Michael upstairs. He's not feeling very well at all. Hasn't slept a wink or eaten." She made a concerned clicking sound deep in her throat. "He blames himself, you know."

"Yes, he told me," Wheeler said. "But I'm sure they've heard from their doctor. About the cause of death. There really isn't anyone to blame."

"Yes, yes. They heard," Aunt Janet said. "But it doesn't seem to have helped Michael. Billy was so young." She led him into the kitchen and offered him a chair. "And bright. He was a whiz at chemistry. He even won an award at school and was supposed to work for a big chemical company this summer. I suppose we should inform the company." Her voice dropped suddenly, her eyes blinking several times rapidly. "Funny the details that pop into your mind. Silly things, I guess, considering."

Wheeler moved around in his chair uneasily, knocking his feet against a table leg.

"Well, enough of that now," she said, her voice perking up. "Can I get you some coffee? Or cake? There's plenty." She motioned toward the cakes and cookies, bread, cheese, and cold cuts that crowded the counter.

"I just had breakfast," Wheeler said.

"Maybe it wouldn't have hit Michael so hard if there were other children," Aunt Janet said. "Billy was an only child, and

48

you know what they say: Only Child, Only Hope. I think Michael feels that way.''

A tall man with a long, straight jaw entered the kitchen and Aunt Janet shifted her attention to him and the empty coffee cup he carried. She bustled to the pot, filled his cup, and even managed to coax him into taking a slice of almond ring cake. Then she looked at Wheeler. "Are you sure you wouldn't like some coffee? Just to keep warm.''

"Okay. That'd be nice.''

"Not that Helen isn't feeling this, too,'' Aunt Janet went on. "She is. She's just trying to be strong for both of them. But it'll hit her once this is all over.''

"I know what you mean.''

"Oh, look at me. Talking away a mile a minute and you're here on business. I'm sorry, Detective Wheeler. I guess we're all a little upset.''

"Please. Don't be sorry. I just have to get some information for my report.''

"You sit there and I'll tell Helen that you're here.'' She moved to the door but paused. "He was a good boy, you know. Everybody liked him so much. I guess there's no place in your report for that, but it's true anyway.'' She left then and disappeared up the staircase.

Wheeler took a sip of coffee and sat back. The predominant color in the kitchen was a creamy yellow—somewhat subdued but fresh, springlike. That plus the spitting ham baking in the oven and the other food gave Wheeler the impression of a normal Sunday.

After a few seconds, Wheeler found himself looking at a calendar hanging on the wall just over his shoulder. He could see that some days at the end of the month had been marked off with shorthand notations. Two caught his attention: *Wm to Dentist* and *Sthport game hm.*

"Detective Wheeler,'' Mrs. Janowski said as she strode into the kitchen. Wheeler rose and reached for the hand she extended toward him. She was much taller than her aunt—almost as tall as Wheeler and yet elegant and controlled. *Trying to be strong* was Aunt Janet's phrase, and Wheeler could feel what she meant. Mrs. Janowski's handshake was firm, her expression direct and composed.

"I'm sorry to interrupt," Wheeler said when they both were seated. "Normally I wouldn't."

"We understand. You have work to do." Her words were spoken softly. "Any way we can be of help. My husband would be here too, but . . ."

"Your aunt mentioned that Mr. Janowski wasn't feeling well."

"Please, go ahead."

"I only have a few questions. . . ." He hesitated, considering how he should refer to the boy. Sensing a formality about her, he said, "About William. Routine information." She nodded for him to go ahead. "William was playing basketball Friday afternoon with friends. I wonder if you know who he was with." He took his pad out.

"Well, there was Steven. Steven Jennings. He's . . . he was one of William's best friends." She looked confused momentarily and said, "I don't recall his address or telephone number. I can get them for you if it would help."

"Maybe we could get that afterward. There might be others."

"Certainly. I should have thought." She gazed down at the tabletop a second and then raised her head. Her long index finger began tapping fretfully on the placemat in front of her. "Let's see. I think Bobby Snow was there, too. They both came to the house yesterday and I assume they were both at the park. I really don't know if there were others."

"That's okay. I can check that out with the boys myself."

"Yes. They'd know for sure."

"About your son's illness, Mrs. Janowski . . ." He wanted the information all right. He'd need it to complete his report on the death. But he wanted more as well. Who her son's friends were. If anyone disliked him. If he'd had any trouble at school or with teammates. Going from the standard questions to these would be tricky. "I wonder if either the Jennings or the Snow boy were aware of it."

"I think they both were," she said. "In fact, I'm sure of it. Both Steven and Bobby were on the basketball team with William, and the team knew." As Wheeler wrote, she filled in the details of her son's history of seizures, where and when they happened. He'd had three seizures at practice. "His coach, Mr. Preston, made sure everyone on the team knew about it and knew what to do."

"Just team members knew, then?"

"I guess others did too. Some teachers. Some other students, the girlfriends of some of the players . . ." Her finger stopped its restless movement. "Is all this information about William's seizures important for some reason? Our doctor called this morning to explain the test results and the seizures were mentioned in that report."

"I realize we're probably going over a lot of the same ground, Mrs. Janowski. It happens. It's the only way we have of putting together as accurate a picture as possible."

"Oh," she said, her finger going into motion again. "It's not that we're ashamed. Or that William was, for that matter. We all tried to live with it as normally as possible."

"I see. And William's friends were used to his having seizures?"

"You never become used to them, but they were familiar with them. He really hadn't had one since he'd been on the anticonvulsant drugs. He'd been taking phenobarbital and Dilantin for over a year and a half."

"So it's possible that a seizure might have been a surprise to them? A shock?"

"I guess." Her finger stopped again. "You don't think Steven or Bobby were there when . . ."

"There's no evidence of that. I simply wondered. . . ."

"They wouldn't just leave him."

"No. I'm sure they wouldn't." But she wasn't really listening to him. She was reconstructing Friday night and what might have happened if someone, anyone, had been there to help her son.

"Mrs. Janowski?" She looked at Wheeler. "I'll try to wrap this up quickly. I know you have guests. Did you know if William was supposed to meet anyone after playing basketball?"

"No one that I know of," she said. "He was going out on a date later and I think he wanted to get home early so he could get ready."

"But did he often go through the park the way he did Friday. Through the north end?"

"It's the shortest route. I think he always took it. Is that important?"

"No," he answered, shaking his head. His questions, routine ones really, had set off a subconscious alarm in her brain. Even her eyes seemed to have hardened slightly, become suspicious. He could tell she was going back over his questions, trying to see some kind of pattern, trying to find out if something had been kept from her about her son's death. To distract her, Wheeler began asking her about her son's school activities, his other friends' names, his teachers. Mrs. Janowski had become guarded and careful now, and these simple questions got Wheeler a short list of people he could contact later. "I think that should about do it."

"I'm happy to help," she said. "I'll try to round up those numbers for you."

Wheeler made an effort to stand, but she was gone before he could unfold his long legs. As soon as she saw her niece exit, Aunt Janet buzzed in, empty coffee pot in hand.

"They drink this stuff like water," she said, filling the pot with cold water and the strainer with fresh grounds. "Nerves, I guess " she added, plugging the pot in. "We all have them. Would you like some cookies?"

"No, thank you."

"On a diet? Everyone seems to be these days. I wish I could lose a few pounds." She looked down the length of her body. "People tell me I'm as thin as a rail, but there's a few extra pounds I wouldn't mind losing, if you know what I mean."

Wheeler smiled at her and she returned it. Then she scooped up the plate of butter cookies and marched off to the living room with fierce determination.

When he heard Mrs. Janowski coming down the stairs, he went out to meet her in the hall.

"Here they are," she said, handing Wheeler a list of neatly printed names with addresses and telephone numbers. After he'd gotten his jacket and moved to the front door, she said, "You'll let us know if anything turns up?"

"Turns up?"

"If you find anything new we might not know about." She glanced up the stairs to where her husband was resting. "The doctor said the aneurysm would have developed even if William hadn't played basketball. Still, it's hard not to blame ourselves."

"When everything's complete, I'll call you," Wheeler said. "I promise. But I think we know pretty much what happened already." He handed her a card with his office and home telephone numbers on it. "And if you think of anything else or have any questions, please give me a call. Any time."

Once he was on the porch and the door had closed behind him, Wheeler took a deep breath of air into his lungs. It was cold and uncomplicated.

A group of people were walking up the street, bundled against the chill and clutching still more pots and baking dishes. Another wave of friends and relatives.

Wheeler moved to the edge of the porch and paused, looking to where the Plymouth was parked and sorting out his next steps. Since he hadn't gotten the kind of information he'd been looking for from Mrs. Janowski, he'd have to spend the rest of the day questioning the people on the list. And where would that lead him? He had a fleeting thought that maybe Gail had been right. Maybe he'd found everything there was to find. That was when he saw the boy standing at the corner watching him.

5

*B*rian couldn't exactly say why he'd decided to go to Wexler Drive. To fix on something real, he figured, something more solid than his flawed memory. It was the same impulse that had made him pull Saturday's paper from the garbage and clip out the article about Janowski.

He halted at the corner of Wexler and Grove and searched for the address listed in the obituary. Number 29. The odd numbers were on the opposite side of the street, and he guessed the house he was looking for would be about midway up the block. The houses all looked so similar he actually missed the number on the first sweep.

Now that he knew where the house was, he wasn't sure what his next move would be. He actually considered going inside; he was that curious about what was going on, what was being said by the family—and whether anything was suspected.

He watched several small groups of people lumber up the front steps, enter, and then reemerge minutes later. A brief stop seemed easy enough. Deceptively easy. Going inside would mean facing Janowski's parents, and he knew he could never do that. He thought about walking slowly by the place once as a kind of silent vigil. A peace offering.

Another group trudged up the sidewalk across the street from him and it made Brian nervous. He'd been at the corner a long time and they might somehow connect the way he was hanging around with Janowski's death. He turned his head so they wouldn't get a clear look at him and let his eyes wander up the line of parked cars.

He spotted the Plymouth immediately. The worn sheen of the brown paint, the tired look of the interior—it was the same car he'd seen outside MacPheason's. The detective's car. He looked back to the Janowskis' house and found the tall man on the porch watching him.

Brian froze a second, staring back, trying to see the man's face clearly, hoping to read what was in his eyes and mind. Then Brian turned around and began walking back down Grove, away from the Janowski house and the man.

He'd gone a few steps when he strained his eyes to the left without moving his head. The man was coming down the stairs, still intently following Brian's every movement.

Brian's glimpse of the man had been brief and faulty, but he was certain he was the same man he'd seen at MacPheason's. The instant the corner house came between Brian and the man, Brian broke into a wild sprint. His stiff legs reached out in long, clumsy strides. He heard his sneakers slap down against the concrete in the same way they had on Friday night, only today, instead of fleeing into the safety of a dark factory complex, he was out in the open on an endlessly straight sidewalk.

He hadn't gone very far when his breathing started to come in short, furious gulps. He told himself to keep going, keep moving his legs. To stop would be an end to everything. A hundred yards down Grove, Brian swerved to his right and dashed across the street.

He leaped between two parked cars on the other side, skidded on a patch of dry grass and, regaining his balance, continued running.

The sidewalk on this side was flagstone slabs, made uneven by the way tree roots had thrust them up at various pitches. He leaped over some smaller ones easily, but his toe caught on a jagged edge and he sprawled head first onto the sidewalk. He struggled to his feet and began moving again, though he knew that fatigue was overcoming him. His legs felt weak, rubbery.

The cold air made his lungs scream with pain. At a large oak, he stopped and turned to face his pursuer.

There was no one in sight.

The man—the detective—hadn't chased him. The street was clear and safe.

Brian spun on his heels and trotted up the street at a calmer pace. Roger was probably right about the cop. He was at MacPheason's and now at Janowski's on routine business—gathering information or seeing if he could be of some help to the family. Nothing more. Still, Brian wanted to put distance between himself and the cop.

He went past four houses and the leaden feeling in his legs returned. He'd have to stop again and this time rest longer.

To his right he noticed a house where the Sunday paper hadn't been taken in yet. If he was lucky, the people were away or still asleep. He went up the gently sloping lawn and over to the corner of the building where a row of short bushes grew.

Once again he checked the street and found it serenely empty. He stooped down, got onto his hands and knees, and worked his way deeply into the tangle of pine-scented branches. He didn't feel safe until he was almost completely surrounded and absorbed into the bush. He waited.

The seconds turned into minutes. His breathing became normal once again. His legs felt stronger and his head cleared. He heard the sound of leafless tree branches moving, a distant airplane passing overhead—ordinary noises that held no danger. He began to feel a little silly hunched up in a stranger's shrubs waiting for some phantom to appear. But he didn't move. The man had been watching him. He was sure of that.

He had almost convinced himself that he'd inherited a little of his mother's paranoia when he heard the wheezing chug of a car engine turning over, and a second later the Plymouth glided around the corner. It cruised up the street slowly, too slowly for a normal ride. Brian leaned forward to see better.

He could tell the driver was searching for something. Or someone. He could see the man's head turning from one side of the street to the other. When the car was two houses away, Brian pulled back and let the branches fill in the space in front of him.

As the car crept past his position, he got a quick, clear look at the driver. Droopy mustache, prominent chin, slightly unruly hair that stuck out in a couple of places where the wind had caught it. But what startled Brian were the man's eyes. They shifted back and forth in a set pattern, coldly absorbing all the details of the terrain. They were the trained eyes of a hunter after prey.

The car passed, receded down the street, and disappeared from sight.

With a loud, relieved sigh, Brian pushed himself to his feet and brushed the icy clots of dirt from his hands. All the while he scanned the street in both directions in case the detective doubled back for a second look. He'd have to think out his every move from now on or he'd end up blundering into the detective again. And the next time he might not be able to slip away.

Abruptly Brian turned and began loping along the side of the house, across the backyard and through a spindly hedge to the yard beyond. Once he was on the street that paralleled Grove, he quick-stepped it to the first intersecting block.

He had to find a phone booth and call Roger. He might have some ideas of what to do.

He searched more blocks than he could count and was close to the main business section of town before he spotted a pay phone. He was fumbling in his pockets for change when he sensed someone watching him and spun around, expecting to find those cold eyes boring down on him again. The street was empty. He went to the phone and lifted the receiver.

Wheeler could have gone after the boy; he could have caught up to him easily. His instincts told him he should have—the way the boy's eyes had widened in alarm, the way he'd walked, stiff-backed and obviously tense. Wheeler shouldn't have hesitated—and yet he had.

Ripples of self-doubt and disgust knocked around inside Wheeler's head. Over seven years separated him from the night he'd killed Willy Jackson, but time hadn't erased the memory. . . .

. . . Jackson and the others fleeing, the chase, the moment he'd fired. The details were all as fresh as when it had happened. Even the months of questioning still stung him—the grillings he'd gone through from the shooting review board, Internal Affairs, the local citizens' committee, and the press. Each had left its mark on him. They were what held Wheeler in place just now while the boy slipped from view.

Wheeler stepped aside and let the arriving mourners pass; then he walked to the Plymouth, glancing toward the corner every few steps and wondering what he would have said to the boy if he had gone after him. The fact that he really didn't know made him wonder if he were reading too much into the boy's actions. He climbed into the car.

Instead of starting the engine, he began jotting down a general description of the boy—dirty brown hair, about five foot six or seven, average build. His clothes were just as ordinary: jeans, blue running sneakers, maroon quilted jacket. There was nothing really distinctive about the boy, but writing down the information allowed Wheeler's nervous anger to subside.

The feeling returned quickly when he finally got the car moving and onto Grove and found the boy gone. He slapped at the steering wheel, cursing his timidity and lack of confidence. The boy had seen him and run off; Wheeler's instincts were correct. This certainty flared and sputtered quickly, a glowing sparkler dropped into water, when he recalled the events of seven years ago in New York.

He remembered the dispatcher's call that night about the complaint: six teenagers were hanging around the front stoop of an apartment building and making a nuisance of themselves. Wheeler and his partner were to roll by the address, ring a few doorbells, and make their presence felt, more to reassure the building's residents than anything else. Calls like this were routine.

Routine. The word left a bitter aftertaste in his mouth, he'd heard it so often during the questionings. "If the call was routine," one of the I.A. team asked, "why did you get out of your car and chase them?"

"They ran."

"Is that all? Did they do anything?"

"It's in the report. I thought I saw drugs. Clear plastic bags—coke or heroin."

"You sure you *saw* drugs?"

"I know I saw a white powder in the bags, and I doubt they were carrying around sugar."

But it wasn't just the drugs. It was the way the kids, six of them, had taken off as soon as they saw the car drawing near. As if something else, something bigger, was going on, or had, and now they had to cover it up quickly. It was so tangible to Wheeler that he'd leaped from the car and given chase even before his partner had fully braked.

He had pursued the kids for about half a block, calling out for them to halt, when the group split, some going straight up the street, others crossing to the right and dodging into a crowded parking lot. Six kids, six directions, and for some reason Wheeler had followed Jackson into the alley.

From behind him, Wheeler heard his partner's shouts to the other boys to halt, mixed with the frantic sound of running feet. A window rattled open and someone yelled, "Get them boys. Get'm."

Wheeler entered the alley then, pulling his revolver from the holster as he turned the corner, and found Jackson waiting, his arms outstretched, holding something that glistened in the shadows. The notion that he was facing down a gun barely had time to register with Wheeler when he dove for the ground, rolling onto his shoulder to cushion the impact, raised his revolver, and squeezed off a single shot that tore into Jackson's chest.

Now, all this time later, driving slowly along Grove Street, the searing instant of the boy's pain and the way he'd cried out, only to have the sound die on his lips, made Wheeler shudder. He glanced to his left and then to his right, as if he were avoiding eye contact with someone. And then there was that awful moment, as his partner and other officers arrived and people swarmed from the buildings to see what had happened, that he'd learned that Jackson hadn't been holding a weapon. Not a Saturday-night special. Not even a knife. He'd simply run himself into a dead-end alley and turned, crouching like one of the life-sized wooden targets Wheeler often faced at the shooting range, and pulled out a metal comb as protection.

A lousy metal comb.

You're trained to operate on instincts, Wheeler thought. You're trained to observe minute details like plastic bags with white powder in them and flashes of metal. You're trained to see these things and react instantly, to think but not to think too much, for if you do, you're sure to freeze up when only reflex action can save you or your partner or a civilian.

He went the length of Grove without seeing the boy. At the first corner he hesitated, wondering whether he might be able to flush the kid out if he doubled back. The thought was insistent, nagging—and yet he wasn't sure how far he could trust it. Deliberately, he made a series of turns that took him away from the area.

Several blocks away, he asked himself, what happens when you find yourself in a situation right out of the police manual, a chase that suddenly turns into a confrontation with the adversary positioned to fire? Only he isn't holding a gun; he's holding a comb. He knew the answer without doubt—you act as trained.

"He's after us," Brian said as soon as he heard Roger's voice. "I saw him."

"Who is this?"

"Brian. I saw the cop again. The one I saw at MacPheason's. I saw him at Janowski's house."

"What the hell were you doing there?"

"I went to see. . . ." he started to say, but stopped, realizing he had no rational explanation for the journey there. "I don't know. I just was there and I saw him coming out of the house. He spotted me."

"Take it slow, Brian. Slow, do you hear?"

"Yeah. Sure."

"Now start all over again. Exactly. All the details."

Brian related what had happened, including the way he'd hidden in the bushes and how the detective's eyes had probed every inch of the street.

"Then you're not absolutely sure he saw you?"

"I'm pretty sure. He drove up Grove as if he had."

"But he didn't chase you right away, did he?" Roger sounded exasperated. "He didn't put his siren on or call for you to stop or anything?"

"Well, no."

"Then it's probably nothing, Brian. I told you the cops have reports to do. It's only natural that one would be at Janowski's."

"I guess so. But his eyes . . ."

"Look, Brian. They don't have anything on us. Even knowing where the beer came from doesn't help them. There's no way they can know it was you who stole it. In a couple of days everything will settle down and that'll be it."

"He's dead, Roger. It's different now. . . ."

"Don't you think I know that!" Roger spat out angrily. "That's all I've been thinking about since I found out." An annoyed sputter of air escaped Roger's lips, and then his voice lowered and calmed. "I feel just as bad as you do. If he hadn't come by or if we hadn't started crapping around . . . well, he might still have had his seizure and all, but we wouldn't be involved."

"It still doesn't seem right."

"I know what you mean," Roger said in a slightly sad and resigned tone. "But it's too late, Brian. Don't you see that? They'd want to know why we took off when he had his seizure. Or why we took so long to tell them. And I'm the one who'll get dumped on the most—go to prison maybe."

"I know that. . . ."

"I'm not sure we're doing the right thing, either. But I can't see any other options except to let a few days go by."

"I guess."

"Good," Roger said. "We'll talk tomorrow at school. Remember, take it slow. I don't think they know anything about us. Anything. I'll talk to you."

Brian hung up the phone but didn't leave the aluminum and glass enclosure. The walls made him feel protected. Sheltered. He needed that just now, especially since Roger, despite his words, had seemed worried and troubled. Brian wondered how he'd be able to get through the following days at school when Janowski's death would be the hot topic of discussion. Amy was sure to say something. His other friends would, too. Just how was he supposed to act, knowing he was one of the last people to see Janowski alive?

Wheeler dried the dinner dish and put it with the others in the cabinet over the counter.

"Here, Susan. You missed a spot." Gail handed a glass back to her daughter. "Near the lip."

"You always see the tiniest bits of gunk," Susan said. She held the glass up to the light. "I can't see anything."

"Look harder," Gail said, turning to round up the last dishes from the table. "It's there."

While Gail was busy, Susan gave the glass a quick, ineffectual rerinsing and slipped it back into the rack.

"This is it," Gail announced, putting the things she'd gathered from the table into the sudsy water. She grabbed a sponge and began washing. "I'll spell you on the washing, Susan, if you'll rinse."

Wheeler asked, "Don't you think it's more than just coincidence? The beer we found and that kid I saw today?"

"I guess it could be," Gail said, adding a little sigh to indicate she was bored by the subject.

"I wish I'd been able to talk to him. If nothing else, it would have eased my mind some." He hadn't mentioned why he'd held off chasing the boy, just that he'd disappeared rather quickly. "Now I have a new wrinkle in the case to think about."

"Make sure all the soap's off," Gail said to Susan.

Susan ran her thumb across the plate. "Squeaky clean," she said, and then, "I told Randy all about what you found. She said she was going to keep an eye peeled tonight for the murderer."

"Susan, the boy died of a hemorrhage."

"And," her father added, "what I have are a few unanswered questions. That doesn't mean that Jack the Ripper is roaming around Edgewater. I thought I could trust you not to repeat anything about the cases I'm working on."

"I only told Randy a little—that there might have been someone in the park. I didn't go into any details. It's true, after all."

"Never mind that," Wheeler said. "No more bulletins to your friends. Okay?"

"I usually never say anything about what you do. . . ."

"What if the boy's parents heard about your 'murderer'?" Gail asked. "Don't you think it would upset them?"

"You guys always gang up on me," Susan said. She pouted quietly for a few seconds and then said, "Okay. I won't say anything more about a murder."

"About anything at all," Wheeler said.

64

"All right. You win." Susan held a fork under the running water for a long time, frowning.

"I'm just trying to find out if anyone was in the area when the boy had his seizure. That's all. It's very dull work."

"You said there was a connection. . . ."

"I said there might be a connection. Might."

"Besides," Gail tossed in, "there probably wasn't anyone there."

"Another expert heard from," Wheeler said. He had meant the comment to come out lightly, even playfully, but for some reason it was delivered with an unintentional barb attached.

"Well, face it," Gail said more forcefully. "You've gone over the photos and reports. You've searched the park and spoken to the deli man. And still there's nothing, right?"

"And the kid I saw today?"

"You said yourself he might have lived on Grove and simply gone indoors before you got onto the street."

The next few moments went by silently, the washing, rinsing, and drying progressing as if in a can that's slowly having all the air sucked out to create a pressure vacuum. At last Gail said, "You know I'm not saying you're wrong or that what you're doing is a waste of time. You know your job better than anyone."

"Well, maybe I can tie up the loose ends tomorrow. I spoke with the kids he was with Friday, so I've covered everybody directly involved."

"I could ask around, too," Susan offered. "In school."

"Oh, no, you don't," Gail said, shaking her head firmly. "This has nothing to do with you."

"It'd be easy for me to ask some kids who knew him."

"No!" Gail looked at Wheeler. "I don't want her involved in this."

"Your mother's right," Wheeler said.

"Aw, nothing ever happens in this town."

"It's my job and I can handle it. Your job is to be a freshman and get good grades and not discuss this case with anyone. Clear?"

"Clear," Susan sighed, drawing out the word to an exasperated groan. "Can I go inside and watch television?"

"Only if your homework's done," Gail said.

Susan turned off the water and left the kitchen. A moment later the sound from the television blasted on.

"That's all I need," Gail said. "Two detectives in the same family."

"She's just carried away a little," Wheeler said. "Once the final report is in, she'll lose all interest in it and go back to thinking of boys. And I'll try to hold it down when she's around."

"Good," Gail said, pulling the stopper and watching as the dirty dishwater drained out. "There's a movie on at nine," she added. "A musical. All we have to do is pry Susan from the tube."

"Sounds good." Wheeler glanced at the kitchen clock. "That'll give me a little time to go over the reports. . . . Don't worry, I'll keep the door closed so Susan won't come snooping around. Call me when the movie starts, okay?"

6

*B*rian grabbed the big wooden door to Harry Truman High on Monday morning and felt a sudden dread that made him pause. Amy or one of his other friends was bound to sense something. He knew where this feeling had started, of course. A couple of times at dinner yesterday, and again at breakfast today, his mother had looked at him in that way of hers that mingled concern, inquisitiveness, and suspicion.

He yanked the door open and plunged into the crowded halls. At first he felt a little numb, hurrying past people and not really looking at anyone. After a few casual hellos, he slowed his pace considerably, though he still wanted to shuck his jacket so he could melt into the crowds. At his locker on the second floor, he began twirling the tumbler hastily.

It was an ordinary action, one he'd performed hundreds of times in his two years at Truman. A turn to the left to the first number, two turns to the right, one full turn to the left, and the lock would open. It was easy, automatic. This time the lock failed to open and he had to spin the tumbler again. His second attempt also failed.

He shook his fingers to make sure they still had feeling, then looked at the number plate on the door. Number 886 was his all right. This time there was a soft, satisfying click as metal teeth slid into position and the door swung open.

He dumped his books and notepads onto the floor of the locker and got out of his jacket. He'd have to get control of himself and fast. The other three were counting on him.

"Hi, Brian," a voice said behind him. On hearing his name, his hands turned cold and clammy. There was no place to hide, so he turned around, only to find Amy standing there, clutching a small pile of books to her chest, both arms wrapped around them comfortably. "Hi," she repeated. He seemed dazed so she added, "Remember me? Amy Baxter. We go out together." She whistled and shook her head. "I know I haven't seen you since Friday, but you couldn't have forgotten me so fast."

"Don't be a wise guy," Brian said. "I was in a fog, I think. Tests and papers and stuff."

"Mondays are like that," Amy said. "Since it's almost time for class, I thought we could go together."

"Yeah. That'd be great." He stared at her.

"You'll need the book," she said. Brian must have seemed totally out of it because Amy reached into his locker, poked around a few seconds, and reemerged with his paperback of *Tristram Shandy*. "If any book deserves to be forgotten, it's definitely this one."

"I guess so." Brian took the book from her and as he did, she gave him a quick kiss.

"Earth to Brian. Earth to Brian," she said. "Wake up, kiddo."

Brian kicked his locker door shut and he and Amy began walking to their lit class, sidestepping idling students as they went.

"I can't say I'm looking forward to this class," Amy was saying. "Timmins is okay, I guess, but he drones on and on all the time."

"Yeah," Brian said, struggling to think of something clever to say and failing.

"And Nancy told me he's going to make us do a ten-page term paper on the book. God!"

He looked at her as they rounded a corner, enjoying the way her cheeks and forehead were gently dotted with freckles and the dark specks of green in her eyes. "Ten pages, no kidding?"

"That's what Nancy said, and she usually has reliable information. I guess it could be worse. . . ."

This isn't right, he suddenly told himself. I shouldn't be talking to Amy about term papers after what happened. That was when it dawned on him that she hadn't said anything about Janowski.

"Brian?"

"Yes?"

"I don't think you heard a word I said." Her lips turned down in an exaggerated pout that seemed upsettingly appealing to Brian.

"I'm sorry. I started thinking . . . thinking about . . ."

"That's okay," she said. The smile, warmer and more understanding, returned. "Nothing worse than talking about a term paper this early."

They halted at the door to the lit class. Standing there with her, he could almost believe what Roger had said about things getting back to normal. Almost.

"Are you going inside, or are you planning to take notes from the hall?"

"I'm going to get some water first," said Brian. "Might help me to wake up. Save me a seat?"

"No sweat," she said, reaching out and taking his book from him. "That's so you'll remember to come back."

He watched her cross the classroom and search out a couple of seats near the window.

There was a water fountain just beyond the intersection of halls and he went toward it, his mind more on Amy than on maneuvering through the traffic. He did a half-pivot to avoid colliding with a kid carrying a container of frogs to a biology lab. His change of direction was slight, just a quick step left, but enough so his eyes darted along the adjoining hall and caught a glimpse of hulking black. He rose onto his toes, curious, and saw a leather-jacketed policeman, his back to Brian, talking with a teacher near the end of the hall.

Brian pulled his head down quickly and hunched his shoulders low, trying to blend into the crowd of bodies. He stumbled along like this a few feet when suddenly his shoulder collided with the wall. He spun to face outward.

"Are you okay?" a pimply-faced kid with glasses asked. "You look like you're going to throw up."

"Get out of here," Brian hissed between clenched teeth.

"I have a lifesaving badge," the kid said. "I might be able to help you."

"Just get lost," Brian said. "And quick."

The kid wandered off, shaking his head and mumbling, "Pardon me for living."

Students flowed by, voices a mixture of laughter and shouts and ordinary conversation. Lockers slammed shut as the last minutes before the bell ticked away. Brian leaned away from the wall and forced himself to study the cop. At least this wasn't the same one he'd seen yesterday. This cop was shorter, stockier. Besides, he had a uniform on, and the one he'd seen at Janowski's was a plainclothes detective.

Impulsively Brian began walking toward the cop. He was about twenty feet away when he realized he was testing himself, playing a game in which he was the only contestant and the only potential loser. To walk by the cop without having an accusing finger or suspicious glance leveled at him would mean the police weren't after them.

He glided right past the cop without hearing his name called out. He felt a certain exhilaration when he zipped into a vacant room, did an about-face, and returned to the hall, this time approaching the cop head on.

He slowed his footsteps, trying not to seem too obvious but wanting to give the cop ample opportunity to see him. The cop was holding his cap in his left hand, gesturing with it to accent whatever he was saying to the teacher. Brian let his eyes scan the man, taking in the details carefully. His uniform was spotless and ironed crisply, his badge a shining emblem. As Brian drew even with the teacher, the cop's eyes shifted to Brian—and just as quickly slid back to the teacher.

Brian felt as if he'd been released from some prison. He could go back to his lit class, sit next to Amy, secure that the tight, trapped feeling would gradually ease. There might even be a day in his future when he wouldn't have any thoughts of Janowski. Yet something nagged at him, a needle jabbing some bit of information deep in his brain.

Around the corner and out of sight of the cop, he stopped and took out his wallet. Carefully he removed the newspaper clipping he'd stuck in with the few dollars he had and began reading it for names. Mr. and Mrs. Michael Janowski, Park Patrolman Jay Fry, Detective Sergeant Robert Wheeler . . . names he'd seen so often since Saturday that they seemed like relatives. There it was. He knew it. Among the first to reach the Janowski boy was Patrolman Arthur Kellogg. Kellogg was the name Brian had just seen on the cop's plastic nameplate.

He put the clipping back into his wallet and hurried to lit class. That feeling of being stalked had returned.

"Actually, it isn't a bad book," Amy said as soon as he'd settled into the hard seat. "Once you get into it. Especially after he dies." She stopped talking and faced him. "You know, I have a feeling you want to be alone this morning. Right?"

"No, I don't," he said. "I'm glad you're here." And he was, more than he could say. Talking with Amy made his troubles seem distant.

"Good," she said. "Then you won't mind if we have lunch together." She smiled at him and he couldn't help smiling back. "That way we can decide what to do Friday night."

Wheeler stood at the office's big window, idly tracing patterns in the frost that had formed near the bottom. He made a random series of dots and ran a line, thin and wavering, from one dot to the next until they were all connected. That was what the Janowski case was, a series of dotlike facts, scattered, seemingly unrelated, and yet begging to have someone bind them together into a complete picture.

He went back to his desk, where his tea had been steeping, and tugged the tea bag up and down until deep red filled the Styrofoam cup. He was looking into his tea as if it were eternally fascinating when the door screeched open and Lieutenant Cummings came in, carrying a wad of papers.

"Morning, Bob," Cummings said. He shuffled through the papers and put a fistful into Wheeler's In box. He left a like amount at Hobart and Conte's desks. "Just a few reports and memos," he explained. "And the Christmas schedule is in there, too. It's the yellow sheet."

"So soon?" Wheeler asked.

Cummings didn't even try to mask his self-pride. "There's a council budget meeting at the beginning of December and . . ."

". . . and it can't hurt to look efficient."

Cummings' smile broadened.

Cummings had been brought into the Edgewater force two years before to take control of the administrative chores and the grant writing. His kind of expertise was generally reserved for larger city police departments, but the town council had felt the pinch of inflation and a decrease in taxes and had tried Cummings as an experiment. Much as it went against the grain, Wheeler had to admit that Cummings had proved valuable— every other town agency and department, including the fire squad, had lost personnel except theirs.

It wasn't Cummings' success that gnawed at Wheeler. It was the man. His personality lacked moods, as far as Wheeler could determine, his emotions finding release in the stream of neatly typed, humorless memos that flowed from his office. Even his body lacked distinction, being neither tall nor short, fat nor thin—and best described as moderately puffy all over.

"Oh," Cummings said, trying to snap his fingers and failing. "I just now remembered. The captain wondered about the Janowski report."

Wheeler gazed at Cummings' oval face and fleshy lips and felt his defenses stiffening. The question was about as offhand as a missile launching. "Did he wonder anything in particular?"

"He was hoping it might be finished today so he could look at it." Cummings paused and added, "The lab reports are in, aren't they?"

Wheeler picked up a manila envelope and waved it in Cummings' direction. "Everything's here."

"Good. I'll tell the captain there should be no problem in wrapping it up, then."

"Well, I can't promise anything. I still have to check up on the kids Janowski was playing basketball with on Friday." He hoped the lie would appease Cummings.

"The mother gave you the names yesterday," Cummings said quickly. Seeing Wheeler's expression harden, he added, "The mother spoke with the captain and asked if anything had turned up. That's all. She happened to mention that she'd given you the names."

"She only gave me a few names, and I had to chase around for the others. I haven't had time to contact them all." Wheeler scowled, shaking his head. "Anyway, I told Mrs. Janowski that *I* would get back to her when I'd finished."

"Don't look so annoyed," Cummings said in that soothing bureaucratic tone that always got to Wheeler. "The Janowski woman belongs to the same club as the captain. The Polish–American League or whatever. The captain was part of a sympathy group that visited the parents."

"I'm still not sure I can finish it up today."

"There's something else behind the captain's interest," Cummings explained. "The *Tribune* is going to run a feature story about the boy's death in Thursday's issue. A reporter's coming to interview the captain tomorrow morning and he has to have a statement prepared by then."

"Another sign of efficiency?"

"It wouldn't hurt if we got a handle on the case quickly."

"I'll try to have it done later," Wheeler said wearily.

"No one's pushing you, you understand."

"Could have fooled me on that one." Wheeler reached for his tea and discovered the side of the cup cold. He stuck his index finger into the tepid crimson liquid. "Damn," he mumbled.

"Look, Bob. You know we want this case done correctly." Cummings shuffled his load of papers nervously and went to the door. "It just wouldn't look good to draw out the investigation, especially one that seems, so far, to be rather cut and dried. We might look confused."

"Or thorough."

"And now the captain has to deal with the boy's mother." Cummings held the door open so that cold air seeped into the office. "She even called him later in the night to check on developments. The captain doesn't need that kind of pressure."

"Okay. I'll try to have it done this afternoon."

"And the captain's very happy with the way you've handled the case so far. The visit with the family showed a personal concern." He tried to give Wheeler a congratulatory smile but let it droop when the younger man didn't look at him. "The boy's mother is happy that you're going into such detail."

"Thanks."

Cummings exited and pulled the door shut as he did.

Wheeler shoved with his right foot so his chair turned to face the window. The frost had begun to spread upward, just about filling the entire series of square panes and obliterating the view. There was only enough clear glass at the top for Wheeler to see that the clouds had darkened and promised snow.

He could write up the report any time now. The lab results would be enough to convince anybody. It'd be simple: type up a neat little form referring readers to the M.E.'s findings on the boy's death and attach copies of the statements he'd gathered from the man who'd found the body, the park patrol, and the paramedics. He could round off the report with the information he'd gotten from Janowski's friends. That would make a neatly tied-up package. Cummings and the captain would be happy, the mother notified officially, and the file stuck in some cabinet to gather dust.

He resisted this, not because he liked doing things the hard way, but because the image of the boy he'd spotted near the Janowski house persisted. It might not be fair to that kid, but his actions labeled him as guilty of something. To Wheeler anyway. And he wanted to find out what that was before he submitted his report.

He turned back to his desk and checked his portable clock. It was almost ten. He was glad he'd anticipated Cummings' pushiness. He was also glad he'd thought to call Kellogg the night before. He'd be at the school by now. Wheeler only hoped the young cop would be able to flush out something interesting.

At first, Susan Wheeler found it hard to ask questions about someone she hardly knew and really didn't care about. Janowski was nothing more than a name to her, and she was sure her voice sounded phony. After several failed attempts, she decided she needed help, so she told Randy.

It never took much to convince Randy to participate in any new scheme, especially when an element of intrigue was present. Soon the two girls were working as a team, going up to kids and discussing Janowski's death with a horrified fascination that put everyone at ease, made them reveal bits of information— how they felt about Janowski or how someone they knew felt about him. Once they had the hang of it, they struck out on their own.

Susan found herself with kids she'd only seen in the halls but never talked to before, diligently writing down every detail she got from them after each interview. By lunchtime, after word of Janowski's death had spread throughout the school, Susan had amassed a small dossier of facts and gossip about the dead boy.

She was in the cafeteria, trying to make some sense of her notes, when Randy appeared with Angela in tow.

"I had to tell her," Randy said immediately, motioning her head toward Angela.

"Randy! I thought we agreed. . . ."

"I know. I know. I wasn't supposed to tell anyone under pain of death. But she figured out what we were up to."

"And you guys think you're detectives," Angela said in a smug tone. "You were so obvious, running around with your pens out."

"I never did that," Susan said, glaring at Randy. "I was very careful about the way I asked questions. How did you find out?"

"Well, okay. I was lucky to find out," Angela admitted. "You both asked Cynthia Cathings the same questions: one before algebra, the other after. Cynthia's no bright bulb when it comes to figuring things out, but I remembered what you said on the phone last Friday night—about a murder and all—and, well, it just made sense that you were investigating the school for your father."

"Nice work, Sherlock," Randy said to Susan. "Anyway, it's too late to get upset. Angela's already got a lot of stuff on Janowski."

"Keep it low," Susan said, glancing around at the neighboring tables. In a near whisper, she asked, "What'd you get, Randy?"

"Most of the girls I talked to thought Jan- . . . er, *he* was a hunk." Randy giggled self-consciously. "Most of the guys thought he was okay, too. But one girl said she was glad of what happened."

"Really!" Susan blurted out. "Did you get her name?"

"Of course." Randy opened her notebook and ran her index finger down a page of scribbling. "Here it is." She looked up and smiled sheepishly. "Actually, she didn't exactly say she was glad he had died. She just said she wasn't all that broken up about it."

"Randy, who is it?"

"Sylvia Serintino. You know, the junior. The one with long black hair and big boobs."

76

"Didn't she go out with Janowski?" Susan asked.

"I think so," Randy answered.

"Definitely," Angela tossed in. "And I heard it was hot and heavy for a while."

"Did you get any details?"

"Susan, I couldn't just ask personal stuff like that. It was hard enough talking about him."

"Try some other juniors," Susan suggested. "If they had a fight that had anything to do with sex, someone's bound to know." She turned to Angela. "Okay, what'd you get?"

"Most of the kids I talked to liked him," she said. "A couple of them thought he was a little pushy. You know, always hitting on girls. Nobody said anything really rotten about him. Here." She handed the list of names to Susan.

"So we're stuck with a bunch of people who say they liked him," Susan said. "A regular dead end."

"Maybe they're all lying," Randy suggested eagerly. "Maybe they all did it. Waited in the park for him and jumped out . . ."

"Randy, that's disgusting. He's dead, remember?"

"Stop being so serious," Angela said. "None of us knew him, and I never even saw him play basketball. And it's not as if there really was a murderer."

"Yeah," Randy chimed in. "I thought we'd have a little fun, too. It's like being an undercover spy—what are they called? Weasels. We're weasels scurrying around collecting information."

"They're called moles," Angela said. "Undercover spies are called moles."

"Whatever."

"Can we get back to business?" Susan asked, rapping the table sternly with her pen. "Do I have to remind you that we're getting this information for my father? And even though he's not sure anything terrible happened to"—her voice lowered quickly—"Janowski, he's not ruling it out yet either. So we have to be extra . . . discreet. You never know who you might be talking to."

"Okay, boss. We'll be good," Angela said. "Anyway, I've been saving the best for last."

She folded her hands on the table in front of her and sat quietly for a few seconds.

"Well?" Susan asked impatiently.

"He had a fight three weeks ago. Right after a gym class."

"With who?"

"I don't know," Angela said. "A guy in my study hall told me about it, but he didn't know who the fight was with. Or what happened."

"That's your big news," Randy said contemptuously. "Personally, I think Sylvia Serintino is a hotter prospect."

Susan glanced down Angela's page of notes. "How come you didn't mention anything about the fight here?"

Angela's eyes shifted nervously along the top of the table and her head lowered. Very softly she said, "I wanted to be sure, that's all."

"Be sure of what?"

"That I was a part of the team. And that I'd get some credit if your father finds anything out."

"Angela!" Susan said loudly. "Thanks a lot!"

"Yeah," Randy said. "What kind of moles do you think we are?"

"Well, Randy made it sound as if you two were the only ones involved and . . . well, um . . . I won't do it again. I promise."

"I hope not," Susan said. "And we're not really involved. Not the way you think. My father doesn't know we're doing this, and I want to keep it that way. Understand?"

The lunch period was almost over and the sounds of the cafeteria, the clunking of plastic trays, chatter, and shouts, seemed to intensify. Susan said, "Let's make a pact. We three will be the only ones on the case—we share all information and all credit. Agreed?"

The other two girls nodded.

"Okay, let's pool our names," Susan said, "so we don't go around questioning the same people three times." She took the separate lists and spread them out in front of her. Angela and Randy moved to either side of Susan and they all copied the names.

"Randy, you check out Sylvia. Angela can follow up on the fight. Remember, we need solid facts. I'll keep asking around about Janowski. I may get lucky and come up with something good."

"Yes, sir." Randy gave Susan a small salute.

"Randy!"

"I heard you. I'll write everything down." She wrinkled her face in disgust. "I'll bet your father doesn't have to do all this boring crap."

"Sure he does," Susan said. She got up from the table, snapping her notebook closed just as the bell rang. "Remember, I never said this was going to be a piece of cake or that we'd find anything interesting. The important thing is that we keep nosing around."

Brian was in geometry, his last class of the day, when a powdery snow began falling. He could hear it brushing against the window, attempting to get his attention. He watched it come down without the joy the first snow always gave him.

He hadn't seen Amy since lunch, and her absence had allowed the disturbing thoughts about Janowski and Wheeler to reclaim him. And with this a new vision arose.

Brian saw himself running down a long, narrow hall of the school, his head twisting frequently to see two figures following. He could tell by the stocky build that one was the cop named Kellogg. The other figure remained shadowed and unidentifiable.

Suddenly the two picked up speed and began closing in on him. Brian kept looking back, to see the shapes looming larger and larger. Then he knew without seeing the face who the second person was. Janowski.

But Janowski was dead, he told himself. The paper had said so. And yet here he was, chasing Brian. He was dead, but he still had a presence, an energy, power to move and act that was more than mere haunting. Brian swung around, determined to outrace Kellogg and Janowski . . . only to find the hall ahead blocked. The chase was over. The game had been forced from cover and driven to the hunter. In front, waiting patiently for him, was Wheeler.

The bell rang and broke into Brian's thoughts. Listlessly he slumped along to his locker and dumped all his books inside. He didn't think he'd be able to study that night and he didn't even want to pretend. He thought of Amy and the few words and glances they'd exchanged that day. They were comforting thoughts, a balm, but not enough to drive away the others. He left the building, cut across the faculty parking lot to reach Deerfield Road, and continued walking toward the business section of Edgewater.

Brian was only vaguely aware of the scenery and the falling snow, his hands rammed into his pockets, when Sticks came up behind him, grabbed his arm, and yanked him off the sidewalk and up a cluttered alley.

"What's going on?" Brian protested loudly, his feet slipping on the slick, damp ground. Sticks brushed past a line of battered garbage cans, hauled Brian around a corner and into an open yard.

"What's your problem?" Brian asked again. He smelled Chinese food and reasoned they were behind the Oriental Mist Restaurant.

"That's what I want to know," Sticks said. "What are you trying to pull?"

"What are you talking about?"

Sticks squeezed Brian's arm hard and pushed him against the side of the building. "You tell me."

Brian didn't say anything, couldn't, so Sticks squeezed again and asked, "What are you and Roger and Al up to?"

"Take it easy." Brian wiggled his arm but the pressure didn't ease. "I don't know what you're talking about. Honest."

"Sure," said Sticks. "I suppose you didn't know that Roger said I'm on my own, did you? That I'm not supposd to hang around any of you anymore."

"Roger said that?"

"He didn't. That flunky Al did." Sticks let go of him and Brian took a step to the side. Sticks said, "And I had this weird feeling that he's been following me, watching me. As if he didn't trust me."

"Al's wrong. The only thing I know is what we agreed to on Saturday. And you were in on that."

Sticks exhaled in one long, frustrated stream and studied Brian's face. "You really don't know, do you?"

"I told you."

Sticks bent and pulled a splintered piece of board from the snow and tossed it at the back fence. It sailed high, missing the target by a foot, and disappeared into the adjoining yard. He stuck his hands in his pockets.

"Al said you'd had a meeting about me and decided I was too much trouble. With my record and the fight I had with Janowski."

"What fight?" Brian wanted to know.

The back door of the restaurant opened, and a busboy dressed in white pants and shirt splattered with an assortment of sauces emerged, carrying two plastic garbage bags. Sticks' back went rigid as the man ambled by slowly, eyeing the two boys but saying nothing. The cans clattered in the alley; then the man came back around the corner and went inside.

Any anger Brian might have felt toward Sticks vanished when he saw the expression on his face. His eyes had a deep, frightened look about them, and the dusting of snow that piled on his shoulders made him seem aimless and alone. Brian asked again, "What about this fight?"

"It was nothing much," Sticks said quietly. "Just a lot of shoving a few weeks back in gym. I don't even remember what it was about, a towel or something stupid. Didn't even come into my mind until this afternoon. Somebody was asking around school about it."

"I saw a cop near the basketball coach's office," Brian said. "Maybe it was him."

"A cop!" Sticks's jaw dropped and he pressed his eyes shut painfully. "Al didn't mention a cop. He said it was a girl. But if the cop knows . . ."

"Don't get upset."

"That's easy for you to say. I'm the one with the record for assault and Roger's the one with a hot-shot lawyer father to cover his ass." Sticks laughed drily. "For all my father cares, I could be in Alaska."

"Nothing's happened so far," Brian reassured him. The back door opened again, this time only enough so a pair of eyes could peer out at the boys. Brian said, "C'mon, let's get out of here."

They left the Oriental Mist and went to a small triangular commons off the shopping district. Once there, they tramped across an expanse of snow-covered lawn to a large marble statue erected to honor fallen soldiers of the Second World War. Two pine trees flanked the statue and spread densely needled branches over, around, and behind it, giving the two boys some shelter from the snow.

As soon as they were inside the protected space, Sticks pulled a pack of cigarettes from his pocket and, after offering one to Brian, lit one for himself and drew in the smoke with a series of rapid breaths.

Brian said, "It's probably nothing. The cop, the girl asking questions, what Roger and Al did." He decided it would be better not to mention seeing the detective at Janowski's. "I'll bet Roger and Al are just scared."

82

"So am I."

"I guess we all are," Brian said. "I'll try to check with Roger and get everything straightened out. Okay?"

"Sure," Sticks said, only to add in an ominous tone, "but something's going to happen, Brian. I can feel it." He inhaled on his cigarette again. A second later his lips spread into a sly smile that turned to laughter.

"Want to let me in on the joke?" Brian said.

"It was nothing," Sticks said. "I was just thinking that you never know who your friends will turn out to be in a crunch. But here we are, Bri. You and me. The dynamic duo."

"Yeah," Brian said a little sullenly. "You and me."

7

*L*ate Monday afternoon Susan cruised down the crowded second-floor hall, quickly scanning the place for Angela. Some help she'd turned out to be.

"Susan," someone shouted from the crowd behind her. Susan looked around, didn't see anybody familiar, and assumed it was another Susan being sought. She went on a few steps, only to feel a tug at her elbow.

"Are you Susan Wheeler?"

"Yes."

The girl talking to Susan was a full head shorter, bone thin, and topped by an unevenly frizzled mop of har. "Angela told me you had a pink sweater on," the girl said. "She gave me your locker number, too, and I was just going there to look for you when I spotted the sweater and decided to take a chance it was you." She took a gulp of air and blinked her eyes. "And it was. Or is, that is."

Susan simply stared at the girl.

"I'm sorry," the girl said. "I guess I should introduce myself before blabbering all over the place. I'm Ruth. Ruth Rathman, but that's too much of a mouthful to bother saying, so everybody just calls me R. R."

"Hi, R. R." Susan said tentatively.

"Well, the long and short of it," R. R. went on, "is that I want to talk to you about the case you're working on."

"Angela told you!" Susan gasped.

"Aren't you helping your father with the Janowski case?"

"I'll kill her," Susan muttered angrily. "I will absolutely kill her."

"Angela said you were trying to find out who Janowski had a fight with for your father. He's a detective, isn't he?"

Susan noticed several heads turning in their direction and felt a nervous blush spread across her face. "Let's talk someplace else," she said quickly, taking R. R. by the arm and pulling her to a nearby staircase.

"I have a lead on the fight and I wanted to tell you," R. R. said. "Hey, did I say something wrong?"

"It's not you," Susan said. She pushed the door open with a sharp jab and led R. R. inside. For added security, Susan and R. R. walked half a flight down to a small landing where no one, either on the floor above or below, could possibly intrude. "Angela wasn't supposed to mention this to anyone."

"Let me get this straight," R. R. said. "Are you working on a case or not?"

Susan hesitated. There didn't seem much use in trying to hide anything from R. R., since Angela had probably already spilled the whole thing to her. "Yes. Sort of, anyway. My father doesn't want us doing this"—her voice got louder and more agitated—"which is why that airhead Angela wasn't supposed to say anything to anybody. The whole school probably knows by now."

"Simmer down, Susan. No need to start frothing at the mouth."

It was obvious that Susan wasn't listening, so R. R. waved a hand in front of her face. "Angela's not to blame," R. R. explained. "I am. I made her tell me." Susan's anger turned to confusion, so R. R. plunged on with her story. "It all comes down to the fact that while I was putting together my article on Janowski . . ."

"Article!"

"Yeah. Oh, that's right, you don't know. I'm the editor of the *Bugle* and I'm doing a little story on Janowski. Anyway, while

talking to some people about him, I got wind that somebody . . .
a girl . . . was also asking questions. Now that's no big deal,
since everybody and their mother's talking about what happened, but I kept hearing about this girl. Are you with me so far,
Susan?"

"Sure. Sure," she managed to say, nodding briskly.

"Well, since the girl was leaving a wide-open trail, I decided to
find out what her angle was. You never know where something
might lead."

"And you found out it was Angela?"

"Easy pie," R. R. said proudly. "And you know what? I think
my reporter's instincts may have paid off this time. I have a
feeling I'm onto something interesting here."

"You're not going to write about us, are you?"

"Sure I am," R. R. said. "Don't you think it'd make great
copy? You know, *Students Aid Detective's Search*."

"No." Susan realized she'd shouted when the word began
bouncing off the cement walls of the staircase, echoing several
times before fading out. In a pleading whisper, she continued,
"You can't do that. Please, R. R. I figured that if we found
anything important, I could tell my father that I'd heard it in the
hall or something. But if he knew we were asking questions
about Janowski"—words failed her and she could only shake her
head mournfully a few times before going on—"he'd be plenty
angry at me. Ground me for a month or two. Or worse."

"But something is going on?" R. R. persisted. "I mean,
Angela told me about the fight Janowski had. And your father
does suspect something."

"Well . . ."

"Well, what?"

"My father doesn't want me to talk about his work."

"You told Angela. And she said there was another girl in on it
too."

"My friend Randy," Susan said limply.

"Look, I don't want anyone to get into trouble. I just want to write something interesting about Janowski." R. R. let this soak in before she added, "I think we can work out a deal here, Susan. You tell me what's going on and I'll tell you what I know about the fight. What do you say?"

"What about the article?"

"I promise I won't write anything about you or your little investigation—unless you turn up something important. I'll even help you. Now you have to admit that's a pretty good deal no matter how you slice it. So what do you say?"

"I don't have much choice, do I?"

R. R. flashed a confident smile that accented her cheekbones.

"Okay, it's a deal. But no story about us asking questions unless I know beforehand. Even if we help him, I'd still have to prepare my father a little."

"Fine by me." This time it was R. R. who did the guiding, leading Susan down the stairs to the basement, where the newspaper office shared space with storage rooms and the furnace. R. R. clicked on the tiny room's overhead light and removed a pile of old *Bugles* from a chair so Susan could sit. Then she leaned against a filing cabinet while Susan told her what she knew.

"So you don't really have much that's solid," R. R. said when Susan had finished. "The stuff about the girlfriend seems like a long shot. I mean, realistically, what could she do to Janowski? I think we should concentrate on the fight. I'll go to the gym and talk to the P.E. teacher about it. . . ."

"You're going to ask him flat out?"

"Sure. People never expect direct questions, so they usually answer them. By mistake sometimes." She handed Susan a slip of paper. "A girlfriend of mine said the kid with the locker next to hers had mentioned the fight. In fact, he saw it. His locker number is on that. You go over and talk to him."

"What if he's not there? It's kind of late, you know."

"Someone's bound to be hanging around. Ask them. And if it makes you feel better, you can say you're on the *Truman Bugle*. We'll meet afterward. Okay?"

"What if I can't find anything out?"

"We know his locker number," R. R. said with a chuckle. "We can always crowbar it open."

Wheeler was just finishing up his official report on Janowski's death when the door opened and the third member of the plainclothes division, Detective Cynthia Conte, came in.

"How do you feel?" Wheeler asked. She didn't look very well, that was for sure—hair limp and straight, eyes tired and watery. Even her complexion seemed paler.

"Rotten," she mumbled, sniffing loudly. She blew her nose and tossed the tissue into the wire basket next to her desk. "Sorry 'bout these wretched sniffles. And thanks for the card. It was nice."

"You sure you feel well enough to be here?"

She sniffed again. "Figured I should get some of the paperwork done before Cummings has a cow." She glanced at the ridiculous pile of papers that covered the top of her desk. "Look at all this," she said. "How can he crank out so many memos?" Another sniffle, another tissue. She looked at Wheeler. "I hope that's more interesting than this."

"Janowski," was all Wheeler said.

"Oh, yeah. I read the thing in the paper about him. Sounded like a nice kid."

"That's what everybody's said." Wheeler punched out the last few words of the report, then pulled the paper from the typewriter, causing the roller ratchets to grind loudly. He leaned back and read the report for typing errors. When he'd finished, he stretched across his desk and handed the report to Conte. "Here. Thought you'd like to see it."

"Yeah. Might make me feel more at home. And, hey, I'm sorry you got stuck with it."

"No problem," Wheeler said. "I'm kind of glad, really."

As she read, he took a memo sheet out and fed it into his typewriter. The official report detailed the known facts of the case, everything seen or said. All lab reports, too. But the official report never allowed room for the hunches that sometimes surfaced.

Wheeler began hitting the keys with his two index fingers, barely pausing to search for the right letters. He wanted his supplemental report to tell what he felt might have happened to the boy, the sequence of events as he saw them. He even found a way to mention the boy he'd seen hanging around the Janowski house.

He paused in his typing and looked up. Conte was holding his report in one hand, studying it carefully; her other hand pressed a tissue to her nose. In a way, his supplemental would have to compete with the M.E.'s findings and the captain would have to choose between them. He didn't see how anyone could overlook the logic of his arguments, especially since getting it down on paper made it even more real to Wheeler. Still, he wanted to be absolutely certain. . . .

He thought of the boy's mother. He might be able to buy a few additional days to investigate by mentioning her desire to know *exactly* what had happened to her son. He finished his memo with a flurry and realized it was already ten after three. Cummings was due in five minutes.

"A real shame," Conte said again when she'd finished going through the file. "Says he was an epileptic since he was seven with a history of seizures. He had . . . let me see. . . ." She leafed through the pages of the boy's medical history.

"Fifteen," Wheeler said.

"Yep. Fifteen reported seizures before the medication took effect. And then this happens." Conte closed the report and handed it back to Wheeler. She said, "It doesn't seem fair. I mean, he's got to fight one thing for years and then an artery goes. It's as if God had it in for him."

They both heard the whistling in the hall and the brisk footsteps at the same time. A moment later Cummings came into the office.

He started to make small talk with Conte, but when a spell of sneezes took hold of her, he moved over to Wheeler, who was putting the file into order and clipping the papers together.

"The captain really appreciates this," Cummings told him, taking the file. "The *Trib* reporter said that a few out-of-state papers might pick up his article. Isn't that something."

"We've hit the big time finally," Conte said.

"So to speak," Cummings answered, either missing or ignoring Conte's meaning. "The Janowski boy evidently attracted a lot of attention as a basketball player. The captain said that Indiana State had approached him with a scholarship offer, and I guess the papers want to follow up on him"—he raised the report and waved it in the air to accent what he was saying—"which is why the captain was eager to study this before the meeting."

"I attached a supplemental," Wheeler said.

"I'll mention that to the captain." Cummings was at the door when he turned, his expression changing completely, turning sober. "I don't know if you heard. The boy's father is in the hospital."

"No kidding," Conte said, disgusted.

"His heart began fibrillating last night and they took him to St. Vincent's just to be on the safe side. Apparently he's going to be okay, but he won't be able to attend the funeral." Cummings looked down at the floor and added, "Oh, by the way, the captain will be attending the funeral as a representative of the department."

"I thought I'd go by the cemetery," Wheeler said.

"That'd be nice. I'm sure the boy's mother will appreciate it." And Cummings was gone, his heels clunking loudly as he headed straight for the captain's office with Wheeler's report.

"Strange bird," Conte said. "You know he sent me a get-well card?"

"Maybe it was a forgery," Wheeler said. "Or maybe he's got the sweets for you."

"Fat chance. I thanked him for the card just now, and he acted as if he'd never talked to me before. Strange." She pulled a fresh box of tissues from her desk and poked the top open. "And do I have to sniffle all over you before you tell me what's in that supplemental?"

After Brian and Sticks separated, Brian went directly to Roger's house on Jennifer Lane. He hoped he'd be able to talk to the older boy alone, one to one, without having Al hovering around. Al might have taken it upon himself to tail Sticks, so maybe Brian and Roger could work out the problem between them.

He trudged the fifteen blocks through the cold and the falling snow, his feet kicking up little white explosions with each step. At the very least, if he couldn't get the four of them together again as a unit, he needed to arrange some kind of truce for Sticks. The look on Sticks' face back there told Brian that, for all his self-confident swagger, the other boy couldn't take the pressure for long.

As he came up Roger's front walk, a curtain fluttered in a second-story window and a figure pulled back from view. Brian had no time to focus on who it was, but the wavy brown hair looked like Roger's.

He rang the bell and waited. There was no answer and he heard no one coming. He rang again. After a long delay, Roger's mother opened the door and said that Roger wasn't home just yet.

Brian left, knowing that Roger had no reason to avoid him. No reason that he knew of, that is. He looked back to the window and wondered if he'd been tricked by the falling snow. The flakes were large and being swirled by gusts of wind.

No, he'd seen the figure. And as this certainty was affirmed, a new, though undefined, anxiety took hold of him. He cursed out loud. He didn't need this additional worry, not with the detective prowling around town after him.

He was thinking all this over when he entered his house.

"No hello for your mother?" his mother said.

"Yeah, sure. Hello." He'd come in the front door, hoping to glide right upstairs to the privacy of his room, and hadn't expected to find his mother sitting on the living-room couch sewing.

"Your sister's in her room taking a nap. I think she's coming down with something."

"Okay. I'll go lightly." He started for the stairs.

"Is it still snowing out there?" she asked. "The window steamed over twenty minutes ago and I haven't seen outside since."

"Yeah. It's coming down pretty hard now."

"Is it sticking on the streets? I'm worried about your father driving in weather like this."

There would never be an end to her worrying, he thought. It was a part of her. "Some streets are covered, but the main ones have been plowed. Dad'll be okay."

"Maybe so, but I hope it lets up before he comes home." She put her sewing on the couch beside her. "I better get supper started," she said, pushing herself up and groaning with the effort. "Got any requests?"

"No," he said. "Can't think of anything." He halted with his left foot on the first step.

"I've got some spaghetti sauce in the refrigerator. And I bought some veal the other day. How about I make some veal Parmesan, hmmm? And French fries. You like the way I double-fry the potatoes, don't you?"

"Sure."

"Sure. Is that all you can say?" She stretched her stiff legs and went to the window to see the snow. "Looks nasty out there," she commented gravely. Then she scurried into the kitchen. "Or I could make mashed potatoes. Which do you want? And I'll make some green beans too. Which is it—Frenchies or mashed?"

"It doesn't matter to me. Whichever is easiest."

"Neither is easy," she called out. "Which do you want is the question."

"French fries."

"Then French fries it is." She seemed pleased by his choice.

The familiar kitchen noises commenced—clunking pots, running water, cabinets being opened and closed, package wrappings tearing. They were comfortable sounds. Brian went up a few steps but paused to listen. It was moments like this, when Patti's chatter wasn't making him exasperated, that he could sense the deep calm beneath his mother's umbrella of concern. He could almost touch her protectiveness.

"You still there?" his mother asked.

"Yes."

"You're awfully quiet. Something go wrong at school?"

Ordinarily the question would have sent his hackles up as one of her typical invasions of his privacy. Today the quiet in the house, the snow falling and smothering all outside, he didn't take it that way. "Looking at the snow, that's all."

"Maybe you'll get a snow day out of this. You could use a little vacation from school, right?"

"Right."

He wanted to tell her what had happened, confide in her and get her advice. Her help. She kept everything in the house—in their lives—running so smoothly, she'd probably have some good ideas. He could ask her for her opinion in a hypothetical way: "Hey, Mom, I have this friend. . . ."

He ditched the notion and went to the window his mother had just left. She'd see through even the most clever ruse in a second, and he didn't think he could bear the disappointment and hurt she was bound to show. He'd just have to deal with the situation—and the detective—himself.

He looked out the window just as a snowplow roared by, the traction chains on its rear wheels slapping the pavement. After it passed, Brian spotted a figure, indistinct and blurry through the wet glass, standing on the opposite side of the street, watching his house. Quickly he wiped the moisture with his sleeve, but the figure had turned hurriedly and vanished into the snow.

His first numbing thought was that Wheeler had found him out. This passed when he realized the figure he'd just seen was much too short. Then it came to him—it was Al.

He wasn't certain, of course, just as he wasn't certain he'd seen Roger earlier. All he'd really gotten was a glimpse of a body shape. Nothing more definite. He wasn't even sure that whoever it was had really been watching his house. It could have been a neighbor out for a walk.

He tried to convince himself that the snow was at fault again, whirling around, forming patterns that were deceiving him. It probably wasn't Al at all, he told himself. And yet the anger that now welled up inside him was real enough.

8

At dinner that night Wheeler told Gail and Susan about handing in the final report and how the case had been closed officially.

The end had been anticlimactic—Hobart had simply come into the office a little before five, given Wheeler the captain's memo, and said, "The captain considered your request for more time, but no dice."

What's more, the *Trib* reporter hadn't even bothered to question Wheeler. Evidently he felt the official report and the captain's statement said everything important there was to say.

Susan couldn't mask her disappointment. Gail said a few soothing words, but not much more and soon had Susan chattering away about her day at school. After dinner Wheeler tried to watch the news on TV, and when that failed to distract him, he decided to clean the snow off the steps and walk. The mild exercise and cold air might do him some good.

He put on a ratty flannel shirt and dug out the old blue car coat with the hole in the left elbow. Since only an inch or so of powdery snow had come down, he grabbed the kitchen broom instead of the aluminum shovel.

"I'm going outside," he called to no one in particular. Both Gail and Susan had sensed his moodiness and fled to other parts of the apartment. "Thought I'd clean the steps."

"But it's still snowing," Gail answered. She was in the utility room, tinkering with the broken vacuum cleaner.

"Wouldn't want the snow to drift and block the door," Wheeler joked. He heard the scrape of a screwdriver along metal, a clatter, and what sounded like a spring popping. When the noise stopped, he heard Gail swear.

"You okay?"

"I thought you were outside." She sounded annoyed, and he guessed she was surveying the scattered remains of the vacuum, trying to figure out which part went where.

"I am now," he said, opening the door and stepping onto the small cement porch.

The night was completely still except for the cottony snow that fell without much purpose. None of his neighbors were out and no cars moved along the street.

He started sweeping, using long, even strokes to push the thin accumulation to one side. Once he'd gotten a mound of snow together, he brushed it into the evergreen bushes below. The porch clear, he began the same operation on the steps. The fact that snow was already beginning to stick on the porch again didn't bother him; the rhythmical whisper of broom bristles against concrete and the barely audible hiss of snow hitting snow was peaceful, serene.

He was halfway down the walk when a sharp triangle of yellow light knifed across the snow at his feet and Susan slipped out of the apartment.

"I'm going over to a friend's," Susan said. "But I wanted to give you this." She glanced around at the apartment, saw nothing, and then handed her father a neatly folded piece of paper. "I couldn't before. Mom was around."

"What is it?" Wheeler opened the paper and held it up to catch some light from the street lamp.

"Careful, Dad," Susan said, gently tugging his arm down. "And don't be angry. It's about Janowski."

"I thought your mother and I made it clear. . . ."

"Everybody was talking about him today and I just listened. Angela and Randy helped. And a girl named R. R.—that's where I'm going now." She held up a large textbook and a bulging

96

manila envelope. "I've got some . . . ah, papers and stuff for her."

"You couldn't have missed what I said at the table. The case is closed."

"I know," Susan said. "But I wanted to at least give you what we came up with. R. R. even found out who Janowski had a fight with."

Her father didn't say anything, but Susan read a hint of surprise in the look on his face, so she told him about their investigation.

"Fights are pretty common," Wheeler said.

"We know. The gym teacher said they happen so often it's hard to keep them straight." She pointed to the bottom of the page. "Anyway, his name's Bartlett, but nobody but teachers calls him that. He's always called Sticks."

Wheeler thought back through the various pages in the files. Neither the name Bartlett nor Sticks had appeared anywhere.

"Are you angry?" Susan asked. His silence seemed to deepen, so she poked him softly in the arm. "Dad?"

"A little. You promised you wouldn't interfere. Remember?"

"Yes. But we really tried to be subtle. . . ."

"Never mind that," he said. "The case is closed and this won't change that. I want you to tell your friends that, too."

"Okay."

"You said that once before."

"I really won't do anything else," Susan said, noting that he refolded the paper along its original lines and slipped it into his coat pocket. "But you've got to admit we did pretty good for a bunch of amateurs."

"Stay clear of this kind of stuff in the future."

"Okay, Dad. I promise." She rose up on her toes, gave him a quick kiss on the cheek, and started across the lawn area. "See you later."

"In by ten-thirty," Wheeler reminded her. "It's a school night."

He watched her walk down the street, her feet leaving a trail of solidly impressed footprints in the snow. What she'd done wasn't right, and yet he could still feel proud of her, of the way she and her friends had done the tedious, step-by-step sleuthing to track down a new bit of information. Another thought clouded his mind; what else remained to be unearthed?

He grimaced, knowing these were the kinds of thoughts that either drove you crazy or gave you an ulcer. It had happened to him after the Willy Jackson shooting. Once a few days had gone by and the initial shock had receded, he had begun reconstructing what might have happened to the Jackson boy's weapon. People had crowded into the alley before the backup police unit could seal it off; it was dark, confusing—it would have been very easy for someone to take the boy's weapon and leave the comb in its place. They might have dumped the weapon in a trash can or stashed it in a basement.

He asked the investigating team to search the alley and nearby buildings thoroughly, question the area residents. When they did and found nothing, Wheeler requested yet another search. It was there, he insisted. He knew what he'd seen. They had balked at this and at all other suggestions he made during the weeks that followed. Even after the departmental hearing was over, he prodded them to open a new investigation. He'd been acquitted, they said. He still had his job and pension, and his record was clean. Why push it?

Why? Because finding the weapon would be proof of his innocence.

Wheeler turned back to sweeping and saw a shadow. When he glanced up, Gail was at the picture window. He raised his hand in a wave, but she didn't return it.

Brian could hear his father hammering in the basement, most likely working on the trestle bench he'd promised to have finished before Christmas. Brian's mother was sitting at the kitchen table sorting the month's bills into categories and humming contentedly. Another regular evening for the Halihans, Brian thought.

"I'm going upstairs, Mom," Brian said from the living room. "I'll be on the phone."

"Will you be long?" she asked. "I have to call Mrs. Romano before nine about the Rosary Society raffle."

"Only a few minutes."

"You're not planning to go out tonight, are you?" His back stiffened at the inevitable question. "You should use the time to study."

"I'm not going out," Brian answered. That must have satisfied her, since no other sound came from the kitchen except her humming.

Brian was about to head upstairs when his eyes fixed on the living-room window, and the image of the figure he'd seen earlier returned. He wanted to go to the window now to see if the figure had come back, but he didn't, sensing that he was falling into the same pattern as Sticks. He couldn't afford to worry about what Al might be up to just then. He had to focus on Wheeler first.

In his room Brian sat on his bed for a while to organize his thoughts. He needed to be sharp now, to be aware of every detail.

A detail like Patti.

He'd accounted for his mother and father, but he'd completely forgotten her. He stuck his head out of his room and called softly, "Patti, you up here? Patti?"

She had slept away most of the afternoon, awakened for dinner, but even then seemed groggy. Still he had to be sure she wasn't snooping around or listening.

"Patti?"

His parents' room was closest to his, so he checked it first. No Patti. Next he looked into the bathroom, but it too was empty. He got to her room and found it dark and quiet. He was about to go on with his search when he saw her tiny shape curled at the bottom of her bed, the covers kicked to one side. He glided to her side and replaced the covers. Her breathing was too regular for her to be faking, so Brian could count her as safe.

Back in his room, the door closed tightly, Brian placed the phone on his lap, the newspaper article open on the bed next to him. He punched out the number of the police station.

At first he had thought about asking for Kellogg, the uniformed cop. But he guessed this would be a dead end; Kellogg simply followed orders. It was Wheeler who was working on, running, any investigation there might be. He had the answers. The phone rang three times before a deep voice answered it.

"Edgewater Police. This is Sergeant Wilson. May I help you?"

"Well, maybe," Brian said, his voice catching in his throat and rising an octave. He coughed and said, "You see, um, I was leaving school and I found a glove and I think it belongs to . . ." His mind went blank and he grabbed the newspaper article. ". . . Detective Sergeant Wheeler. I wanted to return it to him."

"I'm sure he'll be happy to get it back, son," the desk sergeant said. "If you drop it off here, I'll give it to him personally as soon as he comes in."

"You can give me his address and I'll bring it over to him." Brian was poised, ready at the merest hint of suspicion to depress the button and end the call. "It wouldn't be any trouble. Honest."

"I'm afraid I can't give out that information. It's against department policy."

"Oh," Brian said. "It's just that I live pretty far away."

"Well, if you can't bring it in," Sergeant Wilson suggested, "you could always mail it. We'd be happy to reimburse you for the postage."

This wasn't going right at all, Brian thought. He'd looked in the phone book and hadn't found any Wheelers listed and as-

100

sumed the detective had an unlisted number. Now he was getting the royal runaround.

"Are you still there, son?"

"Yes. Yes," he said nervously.

"You know what I just thought might be easier all around? You could leave the glove with the principal of your school and we'll send a car by to get it. How does that sound?"

"Good." It sounded terrible, and again a nervous quiver shook his voice.

"Where do you go to school?"

"William Jennings Bryan. Bryan."

"And your name?"

Brian paused a beat, feeling a trap close around him with the easy way the man asked the questions. "David. David Allworth."

"Okay, David. We'll send a car around tomorrow. And I'm sure Detective Wheeler will appreciate it, especially with the weather as cold as it is. Thanks for calling."

Brian was angry with himself for not getting the information he needed. And he'd been on the phone too long, too. If the police were able to trace calls, he'd be a sitting duck.

He leaned back and tried to think of a better approach. Come on, use your brains, he told himself. That's why they send you to school.

He punched out the number again and when Sergeant Wilson answered, Brian made his voice gruffer and asked for the juvenile division. The call was transferred, and when another voice said hello, Brian immediately began speaking. "My name's David Allworth from Bryan High and I'm doing a story for our school paper on Detective Wheeler. What he does. How many cases he has. Who he works with. . . ."

"Hold on a second," the officer on the other end said. "Sergeant Wheeler isn't in juvenile. He's a part of the plainclothes division. I really don't know what he's working on at the moment."

"I just asked for his division," Brian said, "and they gave me you. Don't you know anything about his cases?"

"I'm afraid I can't help you too much. And there's no one in plainclothes right now, so I guess you'll have to call back tomorrow."

Think of something. Quick. "I was hoping I could contact him tonight. You see, I have to hand in a story proposal tomorrow morning to my advisor. Mr. Timmins. It's for the Thanksgiving issue."

"Gee, I don't know what I can do for you now. . . ."

"It's going to have photos, too."

"I don't know Sergeant Wheeler's phone number off hand," the officer said. His voice trailed off as he searched his memory. "He lives at the end of Gordenhurst in the cooperative, but . . . I know. I'll transfer you back to the desk sergeant. He has the roster and I'm sure he'll have more specific information."

"Thanks."

As soon as the officer put Brian on hold to switch the call, Brian hung up.

A co-op at the end of Gordenhurst. It wasn't very much, but it was better than nothing.

Quickly Brian dialed Roger's number. He wouldn't let Roger in on what he was up to, or even that he'd seen the cop in the hall. All that Brian wanted from Roger was some reassuring words he could pass on to Sticks.

The phone at Roger's rang several times but went unanswered. He tried the number again a half hour later with the same results.

Replacing the receiver on its cradle, Brian fell back across his bed and stared at the ceiling. He knew what Sticks must be feeling just then—alone, with his past chasing after him relentlessly. It wasn't a feeling that he liked. But there didn't seem to be much he could do about it except follow Roger's suggestion—wait it out and it'll pass. Even so, a nagging voice inside him insisted that there must be something he could do.

Wheeler left the broom leaning against the mailbox and went inside. Gail had gone back to working on the vacuum cleaner; he'd have a few minutes to study Susan's notes without interruption.

He dropped his coat on a chair and, passing the room where Gail was working without saying anything, went to their bedroom.

Earlier, when he'd come home, he'd placed his copy of the Janowski case file on a top shelf of the closet, certain it would remain undisturbed for a long time. He retrieved it now, spread it open on the bed with Susan's paper next to it. He sprawled across the bed, one hand supporting his head while the other idly plucked tiny bunches of hair from his mustache. It was a long shot, of course . . . but some thread just might have a connection now.

He pulled out another fingerful of hair, the needle pricks of pain making him concentrate on the information before him. Gail came into the room.

"I thought this was finished," she said coldly. "Or does this have something to do with your meeting with Susan outside?"

"Stop being silly," Wheeler said. He took the statement Kellogg had from the gym teacher and placed it on top of Susan's notes. "The case is closed. Here's my report."

He offered her the report but she didn't take it.

"If it's closed, what's this?" She gestured to the papers on the bed.

"It's a copy of the file. I wanted to glance over it once more, put it in order. And about Susan, she only wanted to tell me what the kids at school were saying about the boy's death. That's all."

"I don't want her involved in this at all," Gail said. "She's just a little girl."

"I don't want her involved, either, and I made that very clear to her. I don't think she'll even be thinking about it after this."

"Good," Gail said firmly. "Now I wish you'd stop thinking about it, too."

"It's my job."

"Not this much, it isn't. This is excessive."

"Oh, Gail. There's no need to be so dramatic."

Gail moved around the bed and positioned herself so her shadow fell across the papers. Wheeler looked up. "I don't like the way you've been driving yourself over this case," she said. "Since Friday you've managed to completely shut us out."

"There's something else to find and only so much time to find it in," Wheeler said deliberately. "And no one else seems to care. I thought at least you would understand that."

"But the department doesn't think there's anything else."

"They weren't there Friday night. I can't expect them to understand it the way I do."

Gail had seen him like this before, absorbed to the point of excluding everything else, snapping at her. She moved out of his light.

"I don't like the way Susan's getting involved," she repeated as she went to the door.

"I told you she's not involved." Wheeler turned back to his papers. "I just want to look these over for a while."

9

On Tuesday Brian was up and dressed before the sun had fully risen. It was the only way he could be sure to slip out of the house unheard and unnoticed. He made his way down the stairs, expertly avoiding the steps that always creaked, and went to the kitchen.

Without putting on a light, Brian scribbled a hasty note to his mother, explaining that he had to meet a friend to go over a biology paper. Biology was his worst subject, so while his mother would still be curious, he was certain the part of her that wanted him to do better in school would prevail. Then he slipped out the back door.

The temperature had dropped during the night and the snow on the back steps and in the driveway had crusted over. Each foot Brian put down crunched through loudly, seemed to echo and magnify like the clomping of a drunken cow. He didn't feel at ease until he was several blocks away from the house—and his mother's hearing range.

A dozen or more blocks later, at the top of Gordenhurst, he hesitated, surveying the long block before going any farther. Just the usual trees and clapboard houses—but somehow different. More menacing. Darker and full of hiding places for Wheeler. Far away, tiny and insignificant, Brian saw what looked like low brick structures. He guessed those were the co-ops.

When he drew near the apartments, Brian found himself with another dilemma. He had no idea where Wheeler actually lived and no notion of where to begin his search. It looked as if there were hundreds of doors, hundreds of possibilities.

He began sauntering up and down the sidewalk, hunting for some clue to Wheeler's whereabouts, all the time alert for any suspicious sounds. If he kept moving, didn't stare too much, no one would take much notice of him. A shudder ran through him, both of triumph and fear, when he located the brown Plymouth parked between buildings.

He circled the buildings cautiously, hoping to zero in on the detective. A few of the mailboxes had nameplates, but most were untagged and uncommunicative.

Instead of standing around in the open, Brian crossed the street hurriedly and walked to the end of the block where an empty lot was wedged between two houses. He could stay there safely, mingling with the rhododendrons and scraggly pines, and keep an eye on the Plymouth. And if Wheeler did happen to see him again, Brian could beat it up the adjacent driveway and across backyards to the streets beyond.

Activity in the area increased as the light brightened. People came out to clear snow from their steps and ice from car windshields. Cars were started. Brian checked his driveway escape route. If there was one thing he'd learned from his first encounter with Wheeler, it was always to have an escape route. It gave you some control over a situation.

A few moments later another door opened, revealing Wheeler. Even though Brian's previous glimpses of the man had been fleeting, he recognized the mustache and sharp facial features immediately. And the eyes. Brian shrank back, his heart pumping blood at a frantic rate.

Wheeler kicked chunks of icy snow from the small stoop and turned to a woman at the door who was dressed in jeans and a light green sweater and hugging herself for warmth. He said something to her, then turned and marched across the lawn section to his car. The woman disappeared back inside.

At the car Wheeler brushed snow from the handle of the door before opening it and climbing in. The engine started and warmed past the point of stalling; he got out and began scraping ice from the windshield.

This was the moment Brian had been waiting for, the one he'd pictured scores of times since the previous afternoon. He was going to test himself again—walk across the street and right by Wheeler in the same way he'd done with Kellogg in the school hall. It would tell him once and for all whether there was a police investigation on.

The door to Wheeler's apartment opened again and the woman emerged, this time wearing a heavy winter jacket and gloves and carrying a snow shovel.

Brian would have to make his move soon or Wheeler would have the car cleaned and drive off. Brian wanted to move, tried to, but his hands and feet seemed rooted. Walking by Kellogg had been easy in the crowded, noisy hall, but this would be different. Just him and Wheeler and no cover to hide behind. And Wheeler's eyes saw everything.

The next instant the Plymouth snorted into gear and pulled into the street, heading away from where Brian was standing. The woman stopped her shoveling long enough to wave to Wheeler and watch the car vanish up the street. Then she leaned into her shoveling again.

Brian found the use of his leg muscles finally, turned, and set off for school.

He'd worried about his plan all night, thought out his moves, the way he'd keep his face impassive. He'd imagined his every step and action—even tried to see how Wheeler might react to him. He'd wanted to turn the tables on the detective, become the hunter and gain some advantage over him. But just seeing the cold resolve with which the man had left his apartment, the quick, jabbing motions he'd used to clean the windshield, made that plan seem silly, childish.

What's more, the determined look in Wheeler's eyes told Brian the answer to his question. Wheeler was after them all right. The only question remaining was how close he was.

For some reason, the janitor hadn't turned on the furnace until after eight-thirty that morning and the air in the *Bugle* office was still dank and chilly. Susan sat on the wooden chair, her coat on, shivering.

"Susan, you know what your problem is? You worry too much." R. R. stared hard at Susan from behind her desk, her face showing mild displeasure. "It's not good for you, believe me. You'll get acne."

"I told you I don't like lying to my father, that's all. I promised I wouldn't mess around in the Janowski case anymore."

"We're not messing around," R. R. said calmly. "I don't see what the big deal is."

"The big deal is. . . ."

"I know, you don't want to lie to your father." R. R. picked up a yellow-feathered dart and tossed it at a dart board on the wall to her right. The dart missed the board completely and stuck in the wall. R. R. sighed.

"It may not be important to you, but it is to me," Susan said, rubbing her hands together for warmth. "I mean, I already went against him once when I started asking around school about Janowski. I even made copies of his reports for you." She shifted uneasily in her chair, recalling how she'd sneaked her father's report from the closet the night before and scribbled down as much of it as possible.

"Exactly, Susan," R. R. said, a new spirit entering her voice. She craned toward Susan. "Don't you see, we've done a lot of valuable work on this already. It would be a shame to just drop it like a cold potato." Here her tone became more personal, confidential. "Look, your father's supplemental report said there was more to find out, so we could be on the trail of something here. Something big. Something . . ."

"And there may not be anything at all." Susan slumped down lower in the chair, feeling the weight of R. R.'s persuasiveness as if it were a hand pressing on her shoulder. "I don't know," she said. "You say one thing. My father says something else. I feel like a ping-pong ball."

"Just hear me out for a second. Okay?" R. R. said, leaning back in her chair confidently. "First, one of our fellow students is dead"—to emphasize her point, she held up her index finger and waggled it at Susan—"second, your father thinks Janowski was hit by someone. Maybe with his own basketball. Third, we come up with the name of someone who's had a fight with Janowski recently."

"You forgot number four," Susan added. "The case was closed by the police department. And since my father knows about numbers one, two, and three, it seems logical that he didn't think the fight was very important."

"But he didn't check it out, did he?" R. R. jumped to her feet with the pronouncement and began pacing beside her desk, deep in thought. After a few turns, she faced Susan. "I think we have a responsibility to follow through on what we started. To Janowski. And since there's no police investigation, we can't get in their way or mess things up."

Susan sank a little lower in her chair.

"I don't want you to do anything that'll bum you out," R. R. went on. "It's just that if both you and I work on this together, we can get it all finished pretty quickly, find out for sure if we really have anything."

"I think my arm is being twisted." Susan scrunched up her face as her mind went over what R. R. had just said and weighed this with what her father had said the night before and what would happen to her if she went against his wishes and was caught. Against her better judgment, she said, "Okay, what are we supposed to do?"

"That's the spirit," R. R. shouted, smiling broadly and scurrying back to her chair. "Here's the way I see it. This Bartlett is the best lead we've come up with. Now your father mentions that there were at least three people in the park drinking beer.

That means there were two other guys there beside Bartlett."

"But we don't even know if he was there."

"Susan, that's our working premise. If we assume Bartlett was there, our next step is to prove it. If we can't, well, Bartlett is innocent and we drop the whole thing."

"Okay," Susan mumbled. "Assuming Bartlett was there, how are we supposed to prove it?"

"We try to figure out who the other kids might be. And we do that by finding out who Bartlett's friends are."

That sounded logical to Susan. And relatively harmless.

R. R. said, "I think the best thing for you to do is go to some of the people you've talked to before. They trust you already. That'll give you an opening to talk about Bartlett. I'll try the gym teacher again." R. R. saw Susan's eyes flutter nervously. "Don't worry. I'm going to tell him I'm working on another story—something about school friendships, how they develop. Once we know who Bartlett's friends are, we check *them* out, find out where they were Friday night when it happened."

"As usual, you make it all sound simple."

"It is. What's more, we can do it without letting on what we're up to. That way, if Bartlett turns out to be clean, nobody'll be hurt and all we're out is a little time."

"What about Angela and Randy?"

"I saw Angela earlier and I think she's a lost cause. She was making goo-goo eyes at some guy in the hall. And I didn't think Randy could be trusted to ask around without blabbing what we're up to."

Susan sat up in her chair and began gathering up her books in expectation of the morning bell. "You're right about that," she said, piling the books on her lap.

"So I sent her off to track down the names of everybody Sylvia what's-her-name has gone out with since her freshman year. Should keep her busy for days."

"You've got everything figured out."

110

"It never hurts to begin with a plan and work it through to the finish. How about we meet back here after school. Say around three-thirty?"

"Fine by me," Susan said. The bell screamed the beginning of classes and Susan stood. "Now I just hope none of this gets back to my father."

R. R. picked up another dart and, after painstakingly aiming it at the board, sent it flying. It stuck with a loud thunk in the wall just above the first dart. R. R. said, "Know what your problem is, Susan?"

"Sure I do. I listen to you."

Wheeler went to the cemetery in the early afternoon, slipping into the heavily wooded grove after all the other mourners had assembled around the grave. He positioned himself behind and to the side of the gathering, next to a fat elm tree. From there he had a clear view of the people and surrounding terrain.

He could see Mrs. Janowski, standing as tall and dignified as he'd pictured she would. As expected, Mr. Janowski wasn't there, but he did spot Aunt Janet beside her niece, shivering despite the heavy coat she was wearing. He remembered her words: "He was a good boy, you know . . . everybody liked him." Well, maybe not everybody.

In the middle of the crowd, barely at shoulder level, Wheeler saw an eruption of white hair that belonged to the captain. The priest made the sign of the cross and began the prayers.

Wheeler was there to show his sympathy, of course, but he was also there to observe. The boy he'd seen on Sunday had been drawn to the Janowski house for some very strong reason—morbid curiosity, concern, as a kind of victory march. Even fear could have drawn the kid to the house.

And there were last night's calls to the station. Both officers had said the kid they'd spoken to had been nervous, and when Wheeler checked with the Bryan High paper, he'd discovered that no article on him was planned. If the boy had gone to that length to find out about the investigation, there was a good chance he'd show up here, too.

Wheeler checked the people at the grave site thoroughly, scrutinizing each young person he spotted. The boy wasn't in the group.

He glanced around at the woods and lines of grave markers, glad of the snow covering that would make it hard for the boy to hide his movements. Nothing stood out to jar the tranquil scene. He was sure the boy would show up. Positive of it. But he didn't.

As soon as the priest concluded the service, Wheeler left the cemetery and went to the station house.

"How'd it go?" Hobart asked when Wheeler came into the office.

"Usual," Wheeler said. "Any word on the boy's father?"

"Captain said his blood pressure was way up. That's all I've heard. Did you see the captain?"

"Yeah. From a distance. He was behind Mrs. Janowski."

Hobart's phone rang just then, and while he handled the call, Wheeler began arranging his paperwork in order of priority. Conte was nowhere to be seen, but Wheeler could tell by the cleanliness of her desk that she'd been able to catch up on most of her late reports. He decided to work on his third-quarter accident and crime figures.

"Did I tell you we got the kids who vandalized the garage?" Hobart said as soon as he'd hung up his phone. "Lady called me just after you went out. Seems one of the kids told a friend and that kid told another kid, who told his mother at lunch. She told me." He shrugged, as if to add "Sometimes you just step in it." "Conte's at the courthouse helping to process the kids. There were six of them. A couple of girls, too."

"That should make the captain happy," Wheeler said. "He can announce the solution of two cases to the papers."

Hobart studied Wheeler silently, uneasy at the way the younger man's lips had set themselves in a straight, hard line.

112

"Look, Bob," Hobart said. "I know you're upset about the captain's decision—the way the case was closed. But it wasn't Cummings or the papers or the boy's mother that decided it. It was your report. The captain felt that you'd gone about as far as possible and turned up everything you could."

"We still don't know who brought the beer to the park. Or how many were there. Or why they left unopened cans of beer."

"I know. But you ran that line of the investigation out all the way and came up with nothing." Hobart shook his head slowly. "Besides, the connection between whoever brought the beer and the Janowski boy is tenuous at best. Even you have to admit that."

"A few days. That's all I wanted. Two days would have been enough time to turn over a couple of rocks and see what's there." Wheeler held up one of the report forms he was working on. "Instead, I'm here doing reports. That's what burns me, I guess. I should be out trying to figure how everything goes together."

"If it goes together at all."

"At least we'd know for sure, wouldn't we?" He found himself growing angry with Hobart—with the way he was willing to settle for incomplete answers. "There'd be no blank spots," Wheeler went on. "No unanswered questions. No doubts. Don't you want to know what really happened in the park?" Wheeler pushed his chair away from the desk with an abrupt shove of his foot.

Hobart said, "You know that we hardly ever find out everything, even if it's only a minor car accident. There's always something missing, left out." Wheeler didn't respond at all, only sat unmoving. Hobart tried another angle. "The captain showed your report to Mrs. Janowski. She seemed satisfied with your investigation."

"The supplemental, too?"

"No, of course he didn't show her that," Hobart said with a touch of irritation. "The captain said she was pleased with the attention you gave the case. Relieved even. You might not be satisfied, but it answered a lot of questions for her and her husband."

"I'm glad of that," Wheeler said as he stood up. "I'm going to take a walk around the building. See what's going on. Have anything that needs delivering?"

"Not now. It's almost four. Give me about fifteen minutes to do the October expenses and we can break for some coffee. My treat."

"Sure."

"You did a fine job on the Janowski case," Hobart said as Wheeler opened the door. "Solid and thorough. I wish you would take a moment to see that."

"I'll try to put it out of my mind and think good thoughts."

"Don't overdo it," Hobart said, chuckling. Wheeler pulled the door closed as he left.

It worried Hobart to see Wheeler so physically exhausted, strained. He wondered if the younger man had picked up whatever bug Conte had had. The halls were certainly drafty enough. . . .

He was about to add up a column of figures when Wheeler's phone rang. He stretched over and snatched up the receiver before the phone could ring a second time. "Detective Hobart here," he said. "No, I'm afraid he's away from his desk just now. Can I help you?" The voice on the other end began speaking rapidly, and as it did, Hobart rose out of his chair. He was standing when he said, "You said this happened in the school? We'll be there in a few minutes."

Hobart slammed the phone down and slid from behind his desk.

"Bob!" he shouted, grabbing both his and Wheeler's jackets and charging out the door. "Bob. Quick."

It was almost three-thirty and time for the meeting with R. R. Susan strolled up the empty hall to her locker, her head spinning.

114

Since leaving R. R.'s office that morning, she'd spent every free moment talking about Janowski and Bartlett. She'd talked so much her jaw hurt.

She placed her texts in her locker and located the paperback she had to read that night. She also grabbed her fluffy ski parka before slamming the door shut and heading for the rear stairs.

Of course, R. R. wasn't going to be pleased with what Susan had found out. For all her talking, she'd only managed to pick up more gossip about Janowski's active love life and nothing about Bartlett. No one really knew Bartlett very well and no one knew whom he hung out with.

Still, Susan had to smile. She'd tried to use R. R.'s fib about doing a story about school friendships, but everybody had seen through that immediately. It worried Susan at first that people knew what she was up to, but after a while she relaxed. It made her feel important; she was the center of a wheel of information with everything revolving around what she knew and what she might do with it. She wondered if her father ever felt like this.

She was near the stairwell when she remembered how chilly it always was beyond the door. She placed the paperback between her teeth and began fumbling to get her jacket on. There was a sudden rush of footsteps, upon her before she could think to turn, and a second later her jacket was pulled roughly over her head and her shoulder was rammed against the door. The impact emptied her lungs of air and jarred the paperback from her mouth.

The door flew open, cold air flooding around her legs. She felt herself being propelled forward and falling at the same time, and she began struggling frantically to free herself, to pull the jacket off her head so she could see. When she reached up, strong hands gripped her wrist and she felt her sweater pulled up and over her head, and at the same time her knees crashed to the hard floor and her head bounced against the wall.

She screamed but her words were muffled inside her dark cloth prison. She struggled again, but her arms were pinned awkwardly. All she could do was begin thrashing her body around, hoping to break the hold of whoever had her. Instead of freedom, she felt something cold and sharp touch the skin just below her ribs.

"Shut up," a harsh male voice hissed. Her wrists were squeezed and she felt herself shoved into a corner with a knee jammed under her armpit. "Quiet."

"Let me go. Let me go, please." She was crying and shaking and trying to talk and gulp in air all at once. "Please, let me go."

The knee pushed harder and more pressure was applied to her ribs. One of the hands holding her wrist let go but immediately seized her kicking legs.

"Don't try to pull the jacket and sweater down," the voice said. The second her arm moved, she felt a painful jab in her side. "Didn't you hear me? I'm not fooling."

"What do you want?" Susan managed to ask.

"I want you to shut up, that's what." The voice came closer to her ear, and she shivered and began sobbing harder. "Stop making noise."

"I . . . I . . . what do . . ." Wasn't there anyone around who could hear what was happening? Wasn't there anyone in the hall?

"This is the last time I tell you, Susan." Her body stiffened when she heard her name. "Yeah, we know about you. All about you."

She tried to speak again, but her side was jabbed by a sharp object and she fell silent. She wanted to struggle more but felt exhausted and trapped, and the warm, humid air she was sucking in under the sweater wasn't satisfying her lungs.

"You ask too many questions," the voice said.

Another, squeakier male voice chirped an assenting, "Yeah, too many, girlie."

"Did you hear what I said, Susan?" The way he said her name made her stomach turn. He made it sound dirty. The sharp object bit into her side and the voice repeated, "Did you hear me?"

"Yes . . . yes . . ."

"No more questions, Susan." The sharp object began moving up her side slowly, inching its way along her skin until it stopped at the base of her bra. She was nodding her head trying to contain her tears and regulate her breathing. She wanted to agree to anything they said just so they'd leave her alone.

"We know where you live. We know a lot about you." The voice went on in a droning, threatening tone, reciting tiny facts about her movements during the last two days so she'd know they'd been watching her.

The sharp object began moving again, this time crawling up her left breast, gently pushing the cloth of her bra up to reveal soft, pale skin underneath. She began sobbing uncontrollably, pleading and pushing herself away from the probing.

"That's nice," the squeaky voice said. "Real nice."

"Just remember this." The object stopped. "We're not going to be so nice the next time. Do you hear?"

She nodded.

"Good. Okay, let's move it, Sticks."

"Hmmm? Oh, sure," the other voice said. He turned and pulled the hall door open. Susan heard the whoosh as the door closed and sealed shut.

"And don't move for five minutes. Understand?"

She nodded again.

"Remember. We're watching."

The door whooshed again. Susan strained her ears but couldn't hear anything or anyone. Still inside the tunnel created by her jacket and sweater, she moved her hand cautiously, reached out. She'd tell her father about this, she thought. He'd find out who they were and then . . . Her hand hit something and she grasped it. It was her paperback book.

"I thought I told you not to move," the voice said, coldly, savagely.

Her body recoiled at the shock of being caught and the anticipation of feeling the sharp object once more. The tears started again. Long, hard sobs that wouldn't stop. She stayed on the floor, face down, crying until her tears didn't come anymore. Even then she didn't move for ten minutes, but remained on the cold floor, shivering. My father will get them. . . . My father will get them. . . .

10

*E*ven sitting on his thick rubber cushion, Captain Weisinski was engulfed by his high-backed leather chair and sprawling desk. He hunched forward, reading Hobart's preliminary on Susan's attack, shifting in his chair nervously, but never looking up at the three men sitting in his office. Wheeler exhaled impatiently and stared out the window. It was only five-thirty, but outside it was already dark and impenetrable.

"John," Hobart said when he thought Weisinski had come to the end of the report. "As you can see, Susan was able to catch the name of one of her attackers. A junior named Sticks."

"Lawrence Bartlett," Wheeler said, his attention returning to the meeting.

"Right. Lawrence Bartlett," Hobart said. "What's not in the report is that I called a family friend—Mrs. Westermeyer—to get some additional information on the kid. She works in the high school administrative office. . . ."

Weisinski's eyes widened noticeably. "Do we have authority to do that?"

"It was very unofficial," Hobart said, a quick smile appearing. "Completely off the record. Anyway, Bartlett's parents only moved here about a year and a half ago, so his file's thin. No real trouble listed. But she did recall the principal mentioning that the boy had had some problems back in Michigan. I wired his home town, and if he has a record that hasn't been sealed by the courts, we should hear by tomorrow noon."

"Good. Good," the captain said, nodding his head gravely.

He turned to Cummings and added, "We'd better get a court order to look at those school records ourselves. Might be more to them than Mrs. Westermeyer was able to see." Finally he swiveled around to face Wheeler. "Mentions that Susan was bruised and shaken up, but basically okay physically. Is that right?"

"Short of being knifed or raped," Wheeler said drily, "she's fine."

"I'm happy about that," the captain said, tossing the report onto his desk. "I can't imagine this kind of thing happening in Edgewater. It's such a small town—home-oriented, friendly. It's a shock to me. A real shock."

"More than that," Wheeler said. "It was completely unnecessary."

The captain looked at Wheeler in silence, perplexed. Sensing what was coming, Hobart put a restraining hand on Wheeler's arm. "This isn't the time, Bob."

"Someone's got to say it." Wheeler shook the older detective's hand off. "This wouldn't have happened if we'd pursued the Janowski case."

"We don't really know that," Cummings said. When he saw the hard, piercing stare Wheeler fixed on him, he added, "Look, I know how you must feel right now. . . ."

"No you don't," Wheeler spat out. "You don't know how I feel about anything. None of you does."

"Bob," Hobart said soothingly.

"No, I'm tired of hearing the same crap, Andy. I know what I felt about the case." Wheeler realized that he'd leaned forward so far toward Cummings that he'd risen slightly off his chair. He slammed himself back into it. "I should have kept at it, that's all. Kept at it until I found the answers."

"We can't say that we understand how you feel exactly," Weisinski said, giving Hobart an uneasy sidelong glance. "But we can try. We all have kids, too, and we've all worked on cases that, well, didn't add up completely. But believe me when I say

120

that you—that *we* did go as far as we could under the circumstances." Sensing he had Wheeler's attention, the captain braced his hands on the arms of the chair and sat as tall as he could. "There was no indication of violence in the boy's death. The autopsy, lab reports, examination of the scene revealed nothing."

Hobart said, "I have to side with the captain on this, Bob. Hold on. Don't get your feathers bent out of shape"—Hobart waved a hand in the air to quell any protests Wheeler might offer—"You know that I agreed with you at the start—there were enough curious elements to warrant following up. And you did spend three days running down those angles. But nothing turned up. Not one firm lead was uncovered."

Wheeler grunted in disgust. "What about Susan? She was warned to stop asking questions. And she heard a name. Solid enough?"

"But she never saw a face," Weisinski cut in. "She can't positively match a face to the name. It might have been this Bartlett kid, but there's a possibility that the attack was a prank—a vicious prank. Maybe some kids wanted to get Bartlett into trouble." He paused, hoping the younger man would see his position. "That's why I wanted this meeting before any action was taken. We have to see what we have and map out our next moves carefully."

Mapping out moves spelled delays to Wheeler. Before another word could be spoken, he said, "We've got some good fingerprints from the beer cans. We could get Bartlett's prints and see if they match any from the cans."

Calmly Weisinski asked, "What reason do we have for bringing the boy in?"

"We'd be wide open to a lawsuit," Cummings volunteered. "I spoke with Jack Warren about this and he said we were on shaky ground legally. We have to move with extreme caution. Those were his words: extreme caution."

Wheeler felt his teeth grinding against each other as he fought to contain his anger. First it was Cummings and the captain. Then Hobart. Now it was Jack Warren, the town attorney. Each added his two cents' worth and built the wall of caution and delay higher.

Weisinski rapped his fingers on his desk top several times, then abuptly stood and went to the window. Looking into the night, he said, "And we're still getting heat on this. Mrs. Janowski called me a little while ago, demanding to know what was going on." He turned to face the others, the annoyance he felt obvious. "That reporter from the *Tribune* . . . what's his name? Gamble. Gambling. Whatever. He called Mrs. Janowski. Seems he's got the same information that Susan and her friends gathered. He even knew about your supplemental report, Bob."

"Susan didn't give out any information," Wheeler said. "She wouldn't do that. Not to a reporter."

"But one of the other girls might," Weisinski said, returning to his desk and heaving himself back into his chair. "The point is, we're on the spot now. Mrs. Janowski. The *Trib*. A few council members have even called to see what's going on. That's why I don't want the Bartlett kid hauled in just yet."

"So what do we do?" Wheeler asked impatiently. "Sit on our hands?"

"No," Weisinski said. "But I want our hands clean when we do move. I want this handled book perfect."

As if on cue, Cummings chimed in, "The captain and I discussed this just before you came in and we think the two cases should be handled separately. That way neither one will jeopardize the other legally."

"Then you are going to reopen the Janowski investigation," Wheeler said hopefully. "Officially."

"Yes. We'll be looking into that again," Weisinski said. He hesitated momentarily, glancing down and fiddling with a pen before returning his gaze to Wheeler. "I've given this a lot of thought since I learned of the attack on Susan. The Janowski case will be reopened, but I want Hobart to take charge of it.

Conte will handle Susan's. If we turn up a solid connection between the two, we'll join them later."

The electric clock on the wall behind the captain whirred loudly in the stilled room. A car honked its horn several times. When the reality of the words finally registered, Wheeler asked incredulously, "You mean I'm out completely?"

The captain nodded solemnly. "I hope you undearstand the position I'm in. . . ."

"You can't do that," Wheeler said, his voice getting louder. He looked around at Cummings and Hobart. "You can't take me off it. We're so close now. And all this hands-off treatment for Bartlett means wasted time."

"I could have sent you a memo and that would have been that," Weisinski said firmly. "I wanted to tell you myself."

"But I've been on this from the start. I was there Friday night. I saw the parents."

"No one's saying you haven't done a fine job," Weisinski continued. "But you're too close to the case. Just look at how upset you are."

"What did you expect me to do? Smile and go back to accident reports?"

"I expected you to realize how it would look if something went wrong and you were on the case. Even something insignificant." Weisinski's expression was unyielding. "The first thing the papers would ask is why we didn't reassign it."

"Ah, Jesus," Wheeler grumbled, fixing his eyes on the worn floorboards, while his brain screamed at the injustice just done him.

An uneasy, embarrassed silence took hold of the room, with Hobart, Weisinski, and Cummings glancing at each other. At last Weisinski cleared his throat noisily and said, "This isn't an easy decision, Bob. But I think it's best for your sake as well as the department's."

"Right," Wheeler replied without conviction.

After this Weisinski and Hobart discussed the way the two

cases would be handled. Since a low profile was necessary on the Janowski investigation, it was decided to restrict it to a thorough review of the files. The only person Hobart would question would be the medical examiner, and that simply to determine if it was possible that the boy had been hit prior to his seizure. Meanwhile, Conte would dig into Susan's attack. Bartlett's questioning would wait until they saw what the two detectives could turn up—and until Cummings had time to check out the legal complications. At around six the meeting broke up and Hobart and Wheeler went back to their office.

The first thing Wheeler did was to toss the file containing all the data on Janowski's death onto Hobart's desk. It landed with a thump, pieces of paper and photos spilling out.

"They were afraid the New York thing would get dragged into the papers," Wheeler said. "Weren't they? All that concern about the cases being tossed out of court was bunk."

"It might have been a consideration," Hobart said. "The papers would have a field day with it if anything got screwed up. But I don't think that was the prime reason you were taken off. I can't see that with Weisinski."

"I wouldn't expect you to. He's your friend."

"Listen to me for a second, Bob. . . ."

"Listen. That's all we seem to do around here. We have meetings and take notes. We write up reports. But nobody does anything!"

"Look," Hobart said impatiently, shoving all the papers and photos back into the folder with a quick, unceremonious flick of his hand. "We all want to get to the bottom of this as much as you do." Wheeler gave him a disbelieving look and Hobart's voice grew firmer. "You may not believe it, but it's true. And you know we want it done so we can prosecute if it's called for. But this isn't New York City. We don't have the manpower to hold cases open for months. And things like the *Tribune* or Mrs. Janowski can add a lot of pressure—enough to foul everything up. All the captain's trying to do is contain this as much as possible so we can do our jobs."

"And so he can keep his."

"Come off it, Bob," Hobart said. "You've been in Edgewater seven years. You know damn well the captain doesn't work that way."

"Maybe so," Wheeler said. "And maybe I've been here too long to remember how a real cop should work." Without another word, Wheeler grabbed his jacket and stormed from the ffice.

They were going to lose time by pulling him off the case, he thought as he hurried to his car. Time they'd never get back, either. Worse, they were losing his insight. Hobart could study the files all he wanted, but he would never have the feeling for what took place in the park. Never. And without that, there was a chance that whoever had attacked Janowski and Susan would slip by Hobart and the others and be lost forever.

The Plymouth ground and coughed when Wheeler turned the key. He had to crank it five times before the cold engine sputtered to life. It chugged away a few seconds and then stalled, giving off a black puff of tailpipe smoke in its dying gasp.

He felt the building tension in his chest and arms and neck, a tightening that made him want to strike out at something. Anything.

His hand was shaking when he turned the key again. This time the engine started and held.

It was obvious that he hadn't lived down the New York shooting even after seven years. Even after being absolved of any wrongdoing. It was still there to be thrown up in his face.

"Damn them," he said out loud.

Well, he'd show them. He'd show them all. He threw the car into gear and sent the tires squealing across the darkened parking lot and into the street.

Brian had spent as much time as he could with Amy that day, walking to classes, eating lunch, talking about teachers and friends and the snow—whatever came to mind. Being with her was like stepping through a time warp to a world where Janowski's death had nothing to do with him, where Roger and Al and Sticks didn't exist, and where Wheeler wasn't stalking him. He could rest there, stop his running.

He'd managed to extend the illusion of peace by taking Amy to ReFry House for a taco and Coke after school. But once she'd left for home, that brooding, trapped feeling took hold of Brian again. Instead of forcing a confrontation with Roger, he'd wasted time fooling himself.

Later at home, he phoned Roger several times but always found the line busy. It wasn't until six or so that he finally got through.

"You're right," Roger said after Brian had explained about Sticks and why they had to talk. "I think we better get everything cleared up. Listen, I can't talk now. Why don't we meet at Pineybrook in a little while. Say by the play area."

Brian was almost out the front door when his mother pounced. "Where are you off to now?" she demanded, sticking her head out of the kitchen. "It's almost dinner time."

"I won't be long," Brian stammered. "Fifteen minutes tops. I'm going to the library."

"Can't it wait? I don't like all this running around you've been doing lately. Leaving early yesterday. Missing breakfast . . ."

"It closes at seven. The library, that is." He took a step outside to show his determination.

". . . Late for dinner on Friday. Bolting your food down . . ." Her litany was interrupted by a crash from inside the kitchen. "Patti," his mother said, turning her attention away from Brian. "I asked you not to play with that milk."

"I've got to be going, Mom," Brian said quickly, sensing his opening and silently thanking Patti for her clumsiness. "I'll run all the way and be back in a jiffy."

"Don't run. The sidewalks are icy. . . ."

He was down the steps a moment later.

Pineybrook was on the other side of town, close to Roger's house, and Brian found himself hurrying to get there, jogging most of the time or simply walking very quickly when his legs grew tired. He wanted to get everything settled, on an even track. In a little while Brian entered the park's south gate and followed a path through the trees to the play area.

He halted, searching for Roger but seeing only the massive wooden climbing towers and ramps and monkey bars. In the dark the constructions were grotesque shadows—a crumbling castle where an enemy could easily hide.

"Brian."

Startled, Brian turned and discovered Roger pushing through a hedge nearby. Al was right behind, marching in Roger's steps and pausing only to untangle his raincoat.

"Hi," Brian said, his voice low.

Roger caught the questioning irritation in the younger boy's tone and said, "I thought it'd be good if Al were here."

"And Sticks?"

Roger shook his head.

"The way we see it," Al said, "we'd be home free if it wasn't for him."

"Sticks didn't hit Janowski. . . ." Brian began.

"He's the one with the record," Al said sharply. "I guess he didn't tell you it was for assault, did he? And he's the one who had the fight with Janowski."

"So you toss him out and then follow him around school."

"I told you on Friday," Roger explained. "Sometimes Sticks bails out when things get hairy. We wanted to keep an eye on him just in case. . . ."

"And he did, you know," Al said, stepping close to Brian. "Right away he started acting crazy." For some reason Al poked a stubby finger into Brian's chest as if he were to blame for Sticks. "He must have called me twenty times over the weekend, worried about what had happened."

"Weren't you?" Brian asked.

The stubby finger rammed into Brian's collarbone. "You know damn well we were all scared." Al's words were shotgun pellets, angry and searing, cutting down any arguments Brian might be thinking of. "But we all agreed to ride this out, and instead Sticks goes weird on us. Even my mother wanted to know what was the matter with him."

"All he had to do was stay calm, Brian," Roger said. "Keep his head screwed on tight, keep his mouth shut." Roger cupped his hands and blew some warm breath into them. "But that's all past history now. Doesn't count anymore."

"Yeah, but maybe if you'd talked to him," Brian suggested, "given him five minutes . . ."

"It wouldn't have mattered," Al said.

"How do you know?"

"Look, we're not here to talk about that," Roger said. "I just want to make sure that we three understand the situation clearly."

"But I want to talk about it. . . ."

Al's fist jabbed sharply at Brian's shoulder and cut his sentence short. Al whispered, "Do yourself a favor, Halihan. Don't talk. Listen."

"Where do you get off. . . ." Another jab, harder than the first, caught him in the chest.

"Ease up," Roger said, pushing Al a little away from Brian. He looked at Brian. "We can still slip out of this. All of us. They don't have any proof we did anything to Janowski. But Sticks has to keep his mouth shut."

"What if he doesn't?" Brian demanded. "What if he tells the cops what happened? He's scared enough to do that, you know."

"I don't think he will. Not now."

"We fixed it," Al said. Even in the deep shadows, Brian could see a smirk on Al's face. "He has to keep quiet or it's his ass."

"What do you mean? How'd you fix it?"

"Go ahead. Tell him," Al said. "Tell him."

"We had a long talk with one of the girls who's been snooping around school, asking questions about Janowski," Roger explained. "We didn't hurt her, but we made sure she got the point. It was Wheeler's daughter."

"You what!"

"She never saw us," Al said chuckling. "Never saw us, but we saw her. Right, Roger? And she's got Sticks' number all right."

To Brian's questioning looks, Roger said, "It's really pretty simple, Brian. I didn't want Sticks getting any funny ideas—you know, he talks and the cops go easy on him. So we made sure the girl heard a name. His."

"You bastards," Brian snarled. "You damned . . ."

Brian never saw Al's fist before it slammed into his breastbone and sent him staggering backward into a tree. Before he could regain his balance, another punch drove into his soft, unprotected gut.

His arms moved, flapped around really, but were only feeble attempts to block the series of rock-hard blows that assaulted his midsection. He looked up at last, vision blurred, legs about to collapse, when Al chopped down on his shoulder and sent Brian to his knees.

"That's enough. That's enough." Roger's voice penetrated the shrieking that filled Brian's head. "He knows we're serious."

Brian raised his head slowly and found Roger leaning over close to him, his face expressionless.

"Now listen, Brian. We're not playing games."

Brian wanted to say something to Roger, to curse him for his betrayal, for the way he'd set Sticks up, for his own pain. He wanted to scream at the self-assured face, but no words formed.

"I didn't want this to happen," Roger went on. "But I'm not about to mess up my life with a manslaughter charge. I just wanted Sticks to know that if anything happens, we're all going down together. Understand?"

Before he could think to answer, Al shoved him with his knee. "Answer him, Halihan."

"I'll talk," Brian muttered. "I'll tell. . . ." His words trailed off as air and strength failed him.

"I don't think so," Roger said. "The cops got one name today, but they know two people were involved. And since Al and I have someone who'll vouch for where we were all afternoon, that leaves you. You and Sticks." Roger stood up and said to Al, "Grab his arm."

Together Roger and Al lifted Brian to his feet but had to hold him up when his legs folded under him. Roger said, "Use your head, Brian. All they have on Sticks for what happened to the girl is his name. They can't do anything with that except ask him a few questions. So you tell him to keep his mouth shut. About everything."

"You, too, Halihan," Al added.

Brian nodded his head feebly.

"Good. Good," Roger said. "I wouldn't want to see anything happen to you, Brian. I like you."

Suddenly Brian felt himself being propelled away from the play area to the path he'd taken earlier. He wanted to break away from the two boys' grasp, but his legs were too wobbly and his head still spun dizzily. He had no other choice than to submit like a cripple being carried up a flight of stairs.

It wasn't until they were about a hundred yards from the south gate that first Al and then Roger released their hold. "Be smart, Brian," Roger called after him. "Talking won't do you any good. Won't do any of us any good."

Brian didn't respond but continued to walk, his legs heavy weights. Roger's voice drifted to his ears again. "We're in this together. To the end."

"We'll be watching you, too," Al said. Then there was silence.

Brian went to the fence that separated the park from the sidewalk and paused, one hand holding the cold metal of the post

130

for support while the other probed his chest and stomach for damage. He winced as his fingers located the deep, sharp pockets of pain that were already making his stomach queasy.

Then he turned slowly to see if Roger and Al were still there. All Brian found was an empty path, dark shadows, and trees that rose above him. There was no one there and yet he couldn't shake the feeling of being watched, trailed.

He swung around but found no relief in the empty sidewalk or street or the rows of houses. Outside the park was Wheeler's territory.

They had him backed into a corner from which there was no escape. Roger and Al behind him. Wheeler waiting in front somewhere. He'd been set up perfectly. That was when Brian doubled over and began vomiting uncontrollably.

11

Wheeler turned off Gordenhurst and bounced up the driveway entrance hard enough to make the tailpipe chirp along the concrete. The car fishtailed slightly on a small patch of ice, but he managed to control the swerve and pull it into his space. He took the front steps in a single leap and entered the apartment.

Gail was at the kitchen table, leafing through a college sociology text of hers.

"How's Susan?" he asked, slipping out of his jacket and tossing it over the back of a kitchen chair.

"I hope you're satisfied," Gail said. She closed the book with a snap and slammed it onto the table. When she looked at him, he saw that her face was red and puffy. "I didn't want her involved and now see what you did."

"Gail . . ."

"Don't try to say this would have happened even if she weren't playing detective because it's not true and you know it."

"I didn't want Susan's help and I certainly didn't encourage her. You heard what I told her at dinner."

"You can't tell me you didn't talk to her about the case last night," she said. Sniffing back angry tears, she pushed her chair from the table and marched to the stove. With a series of quick moves, she pulled the tea kettle from the stove, filled it with water, and returned it to the burner with such force that water popped out of the spout and sizzled in the flames. "I saw you talking to her," Gail went on, turning to face her husband. "And see what happened—she gets beat up and nearly raped."

"Lower your voice," Wheeler said, trying to sidestep the fight that Gail had obviously worked herself up for. "Is Susan asleep?"

"If you cared at all, you would have been here to help calm her down."

"Gail, there was a meeting to discuss what happened. I told you that before. . . ."

"And you told me it would take fifteen minutes, too," she hissed. "That was over two hours ago." The tea kettle began making a wheezing, gurgling noise as the water heated. Again Gail turned her back on Wheeler as she got a cup for herself from the cupboard. She said, "Sometimes I think you're a cop first and a part of this family second."

"You know I have obligations. . . ."

She spun around to face Wheeler. "And one of them is to this family."

"Will you let me finish what I was saying?"

"And you know what else?" she asked, her words filling the room, magnifying. "I think you're glad this happened. Yes, glad, because now you'll get your precious case reopened and you can prove whatever it is you want to prove. I hope you're happy."

The kettle began to boil then, but when Gail went to pour the water, she realized she hadn't put a tea bag in her cup. "Oh, damn," she muttered, putting the kettle back down.

"I would never want anything to happen to Susan. You know that." He thought briefly of telling her he'd been removed from the Janowski case but didn't. Instead, he reached out to touch Gail's shoulder.

"No," she said, pulling away. "No. You wanted something to happen. You said so yourself. Now you've got what you wanted, so don't act concerned. About Susan or me."

"Gail, what do you want me to do? Never get involved in a case? Never tell you or Susan what I'm working on?"

"Don't go putting it on me," she said.

He frowned, moving away from her. "I'm too tired to fight

right now," he said. She stared at him defiantly, and he added in self-defense, "Whether you believe it or not, what happened took a lot out of me, too. I just want to think things over for a while."

"While you're at it, why don't you think about your family a little." She brushed past him and went to their bedroom, calling out as she went, "That is, if you can squeeze us into your schedule." The bedroom door closed with a deafening thud.

Wheeler exhaled loudly and bit back the retort he was going to hurl at her. Their conversation could go on in the same vein indefinitely, each remark circling the one before, chipping away relentlessly to make small, insignificant points. No, he didn't want to waste time arguing. He wanted to think. And plan.

He made himself a cup of tea with the water Gail had just boiled. It would calm him, let him focus his thoughts. The first thing he did was look up the name Bartlett in the phone book, though he rejected the idea of calling the boy that night. Doing that would probably involve his parents. He wanted to talk to Bartlett face to face, alone.

Ideas half formed on how to arrange this, though most of them evaporated before he worked them out and were replaced by a disturbing image of Gail. Her anger had been apparent in her face, but that wasn't what lingered with him now, what kept returning to bother him. It was something else—a shadow in her eyes—that he remembered seeing for months following the Jackson shooting. It wasn't just weariness, but fear. Fear of what, he wondered. Of him?

Don't think of her, he told himself. What he wanted most of all was for the night to be over quickly, for the blush of Wednesday to hurry to Edgewater. However he managed to meet Bartlett, he knew it would push the whole mess into high gear—and to a resolution.

Brian sat on his bed, studying his room, the chips of flaking paint on the ceiling, the posters of sports heroes he'd tacked up a couple of years before, the mess on top of his dresser his mother was always getting on him to clean up. Things he saw every day until they were a part of him. Whatever comfort he found in these objects vanished as another painful twinge gripped his ribcage.

Slowly, so as not to aggravate his side, he got up, clicked off the overhead light, and went to his window.

The sky was clear; a few stars winked at him and a big, full moon hung up there, throwing a curious pale yellow light over the neighborhood. He opened the window and leaned forward until his forehead touched the storm window.

He could make out clearly the outlines of Shendly's house next door. It was older than his parents' house, low-slung, built of outdated tar paper, and sitting on a lot that had no definable shape. When he was younger he used to sit by the window for hours, marveling at how lucky Shendly was to have property loaded with curving hedges, pointy corners, and secret hiding places. Now it just seemed ominous and strange.

A truck went by on the street out front, its big tires splashing through muddy slush, its engine growling. As the truck noise died down, Brian heard the familiar sounds of his father trudging through the house downstairs as he checked to make sure all the lights were out, all doors closed and locked. His father came upstairs slowly.

"Everything okay?" he heard his mother ask. Brian's door was open a crack, and while the words sounded distant, he could still make them out.

"Yes," his father said, accompanied by a noisy yawn. "A long day. Want to watch some Johnny Carson?"

"No. I'm worn out. I think I'm coming down with Patti's flu bug." His mother coughed, as if to prove her point.

"Want me to get you something?"

Brian didn't hear his mother's answer, but a few seconds later he heard the bathroom light click on and water running. By this time, Brian had seated himself next to the window and was listening. He guessed his father was getting his mother some aspirin and a cup of water. His father went back to the bedroom.

"Thanks," he heard his mother say. Then, "Did you notice Brian tonight? He hardly said a word all evening. Hardly touched his food."

"He's in love," his father joked.

"No, I mean it. I wondered if he mentioned not feeling well to you. This flu thing might have gotten to him."

"Stop worrying about him," his father said.

"But he's got to eat to keep his strength up. You know how he's been running around lately."

"And he's old enough to take care of himself, too." His father's voice was gently insistent. His mother coughed again, and when it stopped his father added, "You should worry more about yourself for a change. Brian's fine."

No, he's not, Brian thought. He's not fine at all.

"I wish I could be sure about that," his mother said.

Ask me, Brian thought. Why not ask me what's the matter. He knew he could never just go to his parents and tell them what happened, but if they asked what was bothering him, gave him a little opening, he might be able to tell them.

"Try to get some sleep, okay? Goodnight, hon."

"Night."

A peaceful silence invaded the house after this, though Brian found he couldn't share in it.

He looked out the window again and sighed. If his parents only knew what had happened, what his involvement was, would they still act the same toward him? Would Amy?

Something to his left, a white speck of movement, caught his attention and he stretched his neck to look toward the street just as a man came into view. Wheeler!

Instantly prickles of distrust and fear stung at him, made him pull away from the window. The pain in his chest erupted again, intensified, and forced him to sit perfectly still, eyes closed, until it gradually died away.

When he finally could open his eyes, he saw that the man was only out walking his dog and not the least bit interested in Brian's house. The man ambled down the street until he and his dog disappeared from view.

Just his overactive imagination at work, he told himself. But getting punched until his guts hurt wasn't just his imagination. And being set up along with Sticks wasn't imagined either.

Sticks. Thinking of him made Brian feel guilty. He'd spent all evening avoiding his mother or brooding over what had happened and hadn't called Sticks to tell him about Wheeler's daughter. For all Brian knew, the cops might have gone to Sticks' house already. They might be questioning him at that very moment.

Brian's feelings of guilt deepened when he realized he'd put off calling so he wouldn't be associated with Sticks. He'd done the same thing Roger and Al had done—left Sticks out on his own, believing, or hoping, that the safest thing was to be by himself.

Yet being by himself only seemed to magnify his fears. He saw things in the shadows that weren't there, heard sounds, and suspected the worst. He only wished his imagination held some sort of answer—or some escape.

12

This was the part Wheeler liked best, when all the weaving and crisscrossing lines of an investigation began to come together, when he finally felt he'd gotten a step ahead of the person he was trailing.

He pushed open the Nelson Street entrance to Truman High and was immediately assaulted by the smell of paint. The odor was pungent, fresh, and reminded Wheeler of his own days in school. He had a brief feeling of being a trespasser and considered withdrawing—until he remembered Janowski's body stretched out on the cold ground and the attack on Susan. He pressed on to the administrative office. Whatever offense he was committing was minor when compared to what had already taken place.

He entered the office and found it brightly lit and occupied by several staff members, filing cabinets, and heaps of papers. A young woman near the door looked up from her typing and asked politely, "May I help you?" Almost immediately she became flustered as she remembered Wheeler from the afternoon before. "You're Susan's father," she said quickly. "I'm sorry. I almost didn't recognize you."

"That's okay," Wheeler said. "Things were a little hectic around here."

"You can say that again. How can we help you today?"

"I'd like to talk to one of your students," he said. "His name is . . ."

"Is that Detective Wheeler?" broke in a female voice from inside a smaller office. That would be Marcia Talbot, the principal, Wheeler thought. There was a scraping of a chair and then Mrs. Talbot swept out of her office and glided toward Wheeler.

"I'm so happy to see you again," she said, shaking Wheeler's hand as if he were a long-time friend. "I'd planned to call your home later." She stopped suddenly, looking from her assistant to Wheeler. "I don't believe I introduced you two yesterday. Things were so . . . well, you know. Anyway, I'd like you to meet Jane Simms."

Wheeler shooks Jane Simms' hand brusquely and managed a weak smile. He wanted to get on with this so he could hold to his schedule.

"I guess you're here about Susan," Mrs. Talbot continued. "Why don't you come into my office and we can chat."

"Actually, Mrs. Talbot . . ."

"Marcia."

"Actually, Marcia, I'm here on another matter." He remained rooted next to Jane's desk. Marcia blinked, not quite understanding. "Naturally, I'm concerned about what happened," he added, "but Detective Conte is handling the case officially." As he spoke he glanced at the wall clock, noting that it was half past eleven and that he was running short on time. He'd have to move things along at a quicker pace. "I believe she was here earlier."

"Yes. Yes, she was," Marcia said. "She was checking the hall where it happened, asking about after-school activities. She was very thorough. She even spoke with several teachers. Mrs. Durken for one. And Ms. Silver also . . ."

She mentioned the names of several other people questioned by Conte, including herself, and began going into some of the details. Wheeler felt his jaw tense as the clock's second hand swept around relentlessly, eating up his time. "Um, I don't mean to switch the subject," he said, glancing at his watch. "The case I'm on now . . ."

"Goodness," Marcia said, embarrassed. "I'd almost forgotten that you're on duty. How can we help you?"

Wheeler explained quickly about the vandalism of the Municipal Garage and the six youths they'd brought in the day before. "I'd like permission to talk to one of your students about it. Lawrence Bartlett."

"Is he in some kind of trouble?" Marcia asked.

This was the tricky part, Wheeler thought then. He'd have to go carefully. "No. None at all. I hope I didn't give that impression. As a matter of fact, no one at Truman is involved." Marcia seemed relieved by this news, but Wheeler decided to press on. "I wanted to check another boy's story out. He claims he was with Lawrence when the damage was done. We wouldn't want to press charges against the boy if he really was somewhere else."

"Of course not," Marcia said. "It wouldn't be very fair."

"Exactly."

"And I'm so glad Lawrence wasn't a part of it. He puts on a tough exterior sometimes—a result of the trouble he had where he used to live, I guess. But he's really very insecure."

That confirmed what Mrs. Westermeyer had told Hobart the day before. And since neither Marcia nor Jane seemed to see any connection between Wheeler's wanting to talk with Bartlett and Susan's attack, it was safe to assume that Mrs. Westermeyer had kept what she knew to herself. That had been the one link Wheeler couldn't be sure of until that moment. Wheeler said, "It won't take but, oh, five minutes of the boy's time. I'll try not to disrupt things too much."

Marcia looked at the clock. She hated to pull students from their classes, but there was a long half hour before lunch, and she didn't want to inconvenience Detective Wheeler. Not after what he and his wife had been through. "Jane, could you find out what class Lawrence Bartlett is in and bring him here."

"That's not necessary," Wheeler said. "Bringing him here, that is." He knew his voice must have sounded odd, a little too insistent. Regaining control, he said, "Maybe I can make it easier all around by going with her. It would take less time that way. And I'd hate to unnerve the boy by making it seem so, you know, official. Being ushered into the principal's office to be questioned by the police. That routine."

"I understand perfectly," Marcia said. "Jane will take you there, then."

"Thank you." Wheeler put out his hand and she shook it. "I hope I haven't inconvenienced you any."

"Not at all," she said. "And please give our best to Susan."

While Wheeler and Marcia said their good-byes, Jane had gone through her files until she came to Bartlett's schedule. When Wheeler turned to her, she had already risen from her chair, a pile of forms in her hand.

"I've got to give Miss Wallace these state education forms to fill out," Jane said as they left the office. "Her room is on the same floor that Lawrence's class is."

Side by side, Wheeler and the young woman walked down the empty corridor, their footsteps echoing off the high plaster walls.

"I don't have to tell you that I'm a little scared about walking in the halls," Jane said when they reached the main staircase. "Not now, of course. I mean when I'm alone. I just hope you catch whoever hurt Susan."

"We will."

They were almost to the top floor when Wheeler said, "About Lawrence Bartlett. I wonder if I could talk with him alone somewhere. Might put him at ease."

"Oh, sure." They entered the top-floor hall and Jane steered Wheeler to a darkened room. "You can wait in here and I'll get Lawrence. His classroom is just down the hall."

She clicked on a bank of florescent lights before leaving, and Wheeler saw that he was being parked in a chemistry lab, complete with beakers holding oddly colored liquids, stainless steel sinks, and the smell of burnt sulfur.

Wheeler glanced at his watch. Eleven-forty. He'd wanted to confront Bartlett sometime before lunch, and twenty minutes was plenty of time. So far everything was going just as he'd planned it.

Brian's European history teacher was still droning on about the Middle Ages and the plague years. He seemed to take particular delight in describing the early-morning procession of death carts that traveled throughout the narrow streets of London to collect the latest dead, stacking them like so many pieces of kindling. Brian was glad he was in the back where he couldn't be seen.

"A quarter of the world's population died," his teacher said, snapping his fingers. "Just like that. Imagine."

Brian didn't have to imagine. He knew all about people dying "just like that." It was so real it hurt.

The teacher snapped his fingers again and Brian had a curious sense of the before and after in a spinning instant: his life moving along smoothly one moment—a normal kid trying to make some new friends, do some new things—and suddenly and forever it's changed and can't be retrieved.

And it wasn't just his life that was involved. Friday night would change everyone around him eventually, would reach out to touch more and more people—his parents and sister, Amy, his old friends, his teachers and neighbors. There didn't seem to be an end to the list.

He stared at the empty page of his notebook. And there was Janowski, too, of course. The basketball crashing against his face, his convulsion, the gurgling sound of his windpipe closing . . . Brian would never forget that.

Brian tried to tell himself he had been an innocent part of what had happened, that he'd really only been a bystander, but he knew that was a lie. When Janowski was lying at his feet, dying, Brian had chosen to flee with the others. And once you make a choice like that, you're welded to the action no matter how you try to explain it away to yourself.

142

"Brian," Amy said, touching his shoulder. "Wake up, kid. Class is over."

He glanced around and saw the entire class in motion, some packing up their books, some chatting with each other, most hurrying to leave the room. The bell had rung and he'd missed it.

"Was a little boring," Amy continued. "The lecture. Anything the matter?"

"No," he said. He closed his notebook and clipped his pen to it. "I think I pulled something in my side doing situps." He'd gotten up that morning to find his side a sickly yellow-blue where Al had landed most of his punches, though the sharp pain had given way to a dull throb. "Hurts a little."

"Probably hunger pains. Maybe lunch'll cure your ills."

It was inviting. Already he felt surrounded and soothed by her perfume, reassured by her presence.

"I can't today. Sorry." She seemed disappointed for a second and Brian added, "I really want to, but I have to talk to this guy."

"That's okay," she said, her face brightening. "I'll be in the cafeteria if you have any spare time." She kissed his forehead and spun around, walking easily between the desks to the door. Brian had to fight the urge to follow her.

When she was gone from sight, Brian gathered his books and notepads together and left the room. In the hall, students charged from their classrooms to lockers in a chaotic scramble. Brian moved slowly to his, flinching whenever anyone came close to colliding with him. Somewhere on the stairs, a tall beanpole of a kid finally rammed into Brian's shoulder, twisting his torso slightly and producing a jabbing pain.

The pain wasn't as bad as he'd imagined it might be, though it did start him thinking about what had happened at Pineybrook. Strangely, he found that it wasn't the animal delight that Al took in inflicting pain that he dwelled on. It wasn't even Roger's precise, cold-blooded calculating that lingered in his mind. He'd thought about these things plenty during the night, of course, but gradually these solid images gave way to something without shape or form: Roger had designed a course of action to save himself, and beating up Wheeler's daughter was meant to put the cops onto Sticks and force Sticks into silence. But why beat up Brian? Why alienate him so obviously?

It was only after thinking over his actions that morning that he saw a pattern. He'd withdrawn to protect himself, just as his cautiousness in the halls was meant to protect his sore ribs. And this fear and self-interest had made him put off phoning Sticks yesterday, leaving them both on their own while Roger and Al remained united. The beating had been meant to drive him farther from Sticks.

Ruefully Brian recalled what Sticks had said on Monday. They were a duo. And if they wanted to have any chance of outmaneuvering Roger, they'd have to stay together, too.

A few minutes passed, and Wheeler began tugging at his mustache nervously. He wanted to get on with this before his calm, rational side took hold. He was too close to the answer to think of the rules he was breaking. He stood and paced in front of his chair impatiently, slapping his thigh with his notebook.

The door opened and Jane stepped inside, followed by Bartlett.

Got him, Wheeler thought the instant he saw the kid's face—pinched and ashen, eyes shifting all around the room. Everything about him says he's guilty of something. Jane made the introductions and then left to deliver her forms, closing the door behind her.

Before saying anything, Wheeler leaned back against a long lab table and considered Bartlett. One thing was for sure: this wasn't the kid he'd seen near the Janowski house. Physically Bartlett was taller, and his hair was lighter and longer.

After a while, Wheeler said, "You know why I'm here."

144

"Miss Simms said something about a kid from Bryan High. I don't know anyone from there. . . ."

"That's not why I wanted to talk to you," Wheeler said sharply. He folded his arms across his chest and stared at Bartlett coldly. "I'm here about Friday. Friday in Van Bedford."

Sticks began shaking his head, his eyes betraying his panic.

"And about Janowski."

Sticks' head stopped moving and he swallowed. "I didn't know Janowski. I mean, I knew he was a basketball player and all, but other than that, nothing."

"Come on, Lawrence. You had a fight with him a few weeks back in the gym. Remember?" Wheeler sensed the boy collapsing into his fear. He jabbed deeper. "A lot of students here have told us about you and Janowski."

"That fight was a long time ago," Sticks stammered. "I . . . I hardly knew him. And I don't know anything about Friday."

"That's not what we've heard."

"You've heard wrong."

"Look," Wheeler said, pushing off the table with a quick motion that caused Bartlett to flinch and draw back a step. "Certain evidence links you to Janowski's death. The beer cans, for one thing." This was why you spent hours gathering tiny facts, asking questions, writing every detail down. They all came into the game eventually, especially during a questioning. "You left your fingerprints on one."

"We were in the park in the afternoon," Sticks said, his words tumbling out in a rush. "Right after school."

"We? Want to tell me who 'we' is?"

"I didn't have anything to do with what happened to Janowski." Sticks' voice cracked, jumped to a higher pitch. "I . . . I was at a dance . . . with some friends that night. You can ask them."

"Okay," Wheeler said, flipping the pad open. "Were these the same friends you were drinking beer with in Van Bedford?"

The boy seemed suddenly exhausted, something Wheeler had expected. If you ask the right questions, lean on the person just enough, you can confuse him into a slip.

"I wasn't with my real friends. Just some guys I met."

"You just said friends," Wheeler snapped. "You must have known them, right?"

"Yes, yes." Sticks began clenching and unclenching his fists. "I mean, I was with some guys, but I only knew them a little."

"Did you know them enough to get their names?" Keep him off balance, Wheeler thought. Keep firing at him, and he's bound to slip up. Wheeler said, "Without them there's no accounting for your whereabouts."

"I was just walking down the street and I met these guys, you know. Three of them. And they were okay—friendly and all—so we went to the park to drink some beer."

"You know the beer was stolen from MacPheason's Deli?"

"No. No." Sticks gave his head a quick shake and then grew still. In a firmer, more assured tone, he said, "Hey, I don't know why you're bothering me. I go drinking with some guys. So what? And lots of people have fights in school and it doesn't mean a thing."

"I'm 'bothering' you, Bartlett," Wheeler said, grinding out the boy's name, "because you've been linked with another incident that happened yesterday. A girl was assaulted after school and she heard your name."

"That wasn't me," Sticks blurted out. He'd heard about a girl being beat up when he'd gotten to school that morning, but not much else. "I was home."

"And I'll bet you were safe in bed, too," Wheeler said. "The girl's name is Susan Wheeler, in case you haven't made the connection, and I believe my daughter when she says you were there. What's more, I think you were in Van Bedford when Janowski had his seizure."

"I told you I don't know anything," Sticks said. "About either. And you can't make me say I do."

146

"You said all that before, but who's going to substantiate your story?" As he spoke, Wheeler inched closer to Bartlett until he was less than an arm's length from the boy. He was so close now . . . so close. He had to talk himself out of grabbing the kid and forcing him to admit his part in it all. "Of course, if you just tell me what happened, things could go a little easier for you. And that might help, especially considering what happened in Michigan."

That really registered. And hard. Sticks took a step backward, bumped into the blackboard, and looked all around the room for some sort of help. "Melendez," the boy said suddenly, a name appearing in his racing thoughts from some Spanish book he'd once read. "Carlos Melendez. He's from Bryan High."

"Thought you said you didn't know anybody from there."

"I don't *know* him. I just met him. That's the only name I remember . . . a bunch of Spanish kids."

Wheeler wrote the name down, even asked Bartlett how to spell it. "And yesterday afternoon?"

"Yesterday? Oh"—a pause as the boy searched for another alibi to put the detective off—"like I said, I was home. You can ask my mother."

"Don't worry, I will. Address and phone number?"

Sticks gave him these just as the lunch bell rang and doors up and down the hall opened, releasing students in a rush.

"Can I go?" Sticks edged toward the door.

"One more thing," Wheeler said. "As far as I'm concerned, you're still not clear. Not by a long shot." He waved his notebook under Bartlett's nose. "Until I check out your story, I want you to stick around school."

Sticks grasped the door handle, its cold metal promising freedom.

"And another thing," Wheeler added, "If you do know anything—or remember any other names—you'd be well advised to tell me."

"I don't know anything else. Honest," Sticks said. He

glanced out the door window and saw the hall flooded with people. "I've got to go."

"You can go, Bartlett," Wheeler said without emotion. "For now."

The boy fled into the crowded hall.

After Bartlett had gone, Wheeler released a long sigh. He hadn't gotten the kid to admit anything, but he'd primed him nicely. Backed him into a corner, made it clear that he was a suspect, then backed off a little. Bartlett would think Wheeler would be checking up on his phony Spanish friend. All Wheeler would have to do now was be patient and eventually, like a poisoned animal seeking the comfort of its burrow, the kid would lead him to the others.

Jane stuck her head inside the lab. "All finished in here?"

Wheeler put his notepad away. "Almost," he said.

13

*B*rian placed his books on the locker shelf, piling them neatly according to size. He wasn't sure what he should do next about Wheeler or Roger or Sticks, and putting his locker in order gave him a sense that he was accomplishing something.

His name was called, but he didn't acknowledge it. Chitchat was the last thing he needed. To avoid whoever it was, he lowered his head and concentrated on sticking random pieces of paper back into his looseleaf folder.

"Brian." Sticks weaved around a clump of kids, sliding on the polished floor, and grabbed Brian's arm for balance. "He's here, Brian. He knows about us. About everything."

"Who knows?"

"Wheeler," Sticks whispered, glancing all around, as if mention of the name would make the man materialize.

"Are you sure?"

"He pulled me out of class. He knows"—his voice lowered, became insistent—"about the beer, the park. And you know that girl who got beat up yesterday. It was his daughter. . . ."

"I know," Brian said, cutting off the other boy's words. He shut his eyes, his face contorting in a pained grimace as the vision of Wheeler stalking him returned, intensified by his real proximity. "I know," he repeated weakly.

"You know? Well, we've got to do something, Brian. Before it's too late. We've got to do something."

"There's not much we can do," Brian said. "If he's here and he knows everything, we're cooked."

"But I've got a plan. I've been thinking about it since I heard about Janowski. . . ."

"No. No," Brian said, shaking his head. "No more plans."

"Just hear me out," Sticks pleaded. He touched Brian on the arm. "Give me ten minutes, that's all. What harm can it do?"

"Hey, Brian," a boy said, opening the locker next to Brian's and tossing his books inside. "How are things going with you and Amy?"

"Fine," Brian answered, nodding his head vigorously. "Everything's fine."

"Glad to hear it. She's a nice kid." He closed the locker door with a bang and was gone, melting into the flow of people headed for the cafeteria.

"Ten minutes," Sticks said immediately. Once again he looked up and down the hall nervously. "Brian, you're the only one I can count on now."

He really didn't want to hear about any more plans. He just wanted to wait for whatever was going to happen. And yet, Sticks was right—Sticks had no one else to talk to. At last Brian said, "I'll listen. But I won't promise anything."

"Great. That's all I'm asking," Sticks said. "You mind if we get out of the building? With Wheeler here . . ."

He didn't have to finish the sentence. Brian knew all too well how it felt to be trailed. He glanced around, half expecting to find either Wheeler or Al hiding among the other students. When he didn't, he grabbed his jacket from the hook and the two of them headed for the exit.

Wheeler traded small talk with Jane Simms for a few moments, giving Bartlett time to get a head start. Like a fisherman playing out line to a hooked trout, he'd have to allow the kid room to move and make decisions—but not too much room.

He said a hasty good-bye, then strode up the hall, away from the staircase he'd seen Bartlett take. If the kid was hanging around, watching, then seeing Wheeler wandering in the opposite direction would give him a false sense of security. Besides, the school's floor plan, a giant T-shape with wide, well-lighted halls, made it easy to observe large areas from the various landings.

Wheeler went to a rear staircase and quickly descended to the next landing. Hanging back a little from the glass door, he stood, scanning the hall.

Where is he? Wheeler wondered, his jaw tightening with anticipation. He couldn't have gotten very far.

When a teacher came in his direction, evidently heading for one of the classrooms on the floor, Wheeler pulled back into the shadows. He could ignore the questioning glances of the students, but not an adult's. As soon as the teacher was gone, Wheeler moved back into position.

He's here somewhere. He might be hiding in a bathroom or in one of the rooms, but he's here. Wheeler was about to hustle down to the next floor when students at the far end of the hall moved aside and a triumphant surge swept through him. There was Bartlett, and he was talking excitedly to someone. As the other boy's head turned and revealed his profile, something else registered. Bartlett was talking with the kid Wheeler had seen near the Janowski house.

The second boy fumbled into his jacket as he kicked his locker shut, and he and Bartlett began moving away. He had two of them now, Wheeler thought. And they'd lead him to the others.

Wheeler pushed on the glass door, eager to stay as close to the two as possible. The door wouldn't open. He pushed again, more frantically, rattling the door jamb.

"It's a pull."

"What?" Wheeler asked, finding a short, dark-haired girl next to him, her face partially concealed by the huge box she was clutching.

"The handle," she said, her eyes darting in its direction. "You have to pull it to open the door. I don't know why they did it that way. Most of the doors are the push types. . . ."

"Thanks," Wheeler said, yanking the door open and jogging off toward the far staircase.

"That's okay," the girl said as the door slammed shut in front of her, leaving her stranded until the next person happened along.

At the top of the opposite stairs Wheeler halted, leaning over the banister cautiously. Better to spend a few seconds checking than to run smack into them and lose the chance to get the whole group. They were nowhere in sight, so he hurried down to the next floor.

Once he was there, no faces stuck out. No shapes looked familiar. Bartlett and the other boy had been absorbed into the lunchtime confusion.

He went down the hall to the cafeteria and looked inside. It'd be next to impossible to spot either kid in that mess of bodies, but Wheeler lingered anyway, hoping a bit of luck would come his way. When it didn't, he checked all the rooms on the floor.

The two boys had managed to slip away. Each empty room and unfamiliar face confirmed that, seemed to mock his earlier hope of a quick, total resolution. But at least he'd discovered another bit of the puzzle—the second boy. He hurried upstairs to the boy's locker.

"Do you know Lawrence Bartlett?" he asked a girl several lockers away.

"No," she said, her hair swirling around, bouncing off her cheeks and nose as she shook her head.

"Well, do you know who has this locker?"

Her hair fell straight down as her head stopped moving. She looked at Wheeler suspiciously. "Why do you want to know?"

"Just answer the question," he demanded. Why did everyone have to question his actions? The girl simply continued to study him in silence, so he added, "Look, I'm a detective and it's important I know who he is."

She shrugged her shoulders and turned away.

"Jesus," Wheeler muttered. He stopped a boy walking past. "Do you know who has this locker?"

152

"No," the boy said. "I'm from another floor."

"Doesn't anybody know who has this locker? It's very important that I find him."

A ring of passersby gathered to see what was going on, but no one seemed to know who belonged to locker 886. Wheeler looked around, glaring, then pushed his way through the crowd. "Thanks for nothing," he said.

Now he'd have to think up a way to get the boy's name without causing Mrs. Talbot to become suspicious.

There were always delays, he thought. But at least he knew who two of the kids were, and nothing could stop him now.

R. R. looked at her watch and saw that lunch was almost over. She went to the pay phone on the floor and dialed Susan's number. Once again, the ringing went unanswered.

Back in her office, R. R. began going through the Janowski case file for the umpteenth time, stopping here and there to decipher a badly scribbled word. Maybe it was all the squinting she was doing that made the words stand out, started the notion forming.

She glanced over the medical examiner's description of the bruise on Janowski's face, then checked Bartlett's file. That didn't add up to anything, so R. R. turned to the files she'd managed to get on Bartlett's friends. She'd only come up with two names so far, Roger Peterson and Alan Kendall. As soon as she opened Peterson's file she found what she was looking for.

"Hot damn," she shouted, clapping her hands in triumph. Seeing Peterson's name in print started her thinking of something else. When Randy had brought in her list of Sylvia Serintino's ex-boyfriends, she had insisted on reading off the names. R. R. pushed aside the papers on her desk, searching for the list.

There! At the top of the long list, just before Janowski's name, was the name Roger Peterson. Coincidence was one thing, but this was too much.

R. R. bolted out of her seat and went to the phone again. She actually had a few digits of the *Tribune*'s number dialed when she thought better of it. She'd gone out of her way to talk to the reporter covering Janowski's death, a Mark Gambling, even read him the important parts of the police reports, and what did he do in return? Nothing, aside from saying, "You've done real good there, honey. Real good."

She hit the receiver lever and retrieved her dime. Get your own information, honey. The dime in the phone again, she fumbled through her jeans pockets for Conte's card.

She wouldn't exactly say that Detective Conte had been nice to her when they'd talked the night before. Fact was, Conte chewed her out for meddling in a police investigation. But at least Conte hadn't been patronizing like Gambling.

"Detective Conte here."

"Hi," R. R. said. "This is Ruth . . . R. R. You know, from Truman High."

"Oh, yeah. Hi." She sounded wary. "Can I help you with anything?"

"I was just reading over the reports again, and I think I found something interesting."

Conte said something inaudible under her breath. When she spoke, she could barely contain her anger. "Didn't I make it clear that I didn't want you mucking around in the case—any case—anymore? Wasn't Susan's getting attacked enough to convince you?"

"I was only going over the stuff in my office," R. R. said, making her voice apologetic. She paused for effect. "I only thought I could help." Another pause.

"Okay, R. R. Okay." Conte sighed loudly. "It's been pretty hectic here this morning and I tend to get grumpy. So what did you find this time."

R. R. made a quick check behind her to be sure the stairs and hall were empty. "The report says that Janowski had a bruise on the right side of his face."

"We know that already."

154

"Don't you see? If he was hit by a basketball, it had to be done by someone facing him. And to get a bruise on his right side, Janowski would have to have been hit by a lefty."

There was a moment of silence from Conte's end. Then she said, "That's very interesting. But what does that get us?"

"Well, it says in Bartlett's student file that he's right-handed, so that lets him off. He might have been in the park when it happened, of course."

"I'm almost afraid to ask," Conte interrupted. "But how did you come by Bartlett's file? I'm still waiting for a court order to see it."

"Oh," R. R. said. "A friend of mine does typing for the office. For credit. Anyway, she made me the copy."

"I get the picture. Okay, so a lefty might have done it, but that doesn't tell us who. There are a lot of left-handed people in the world."

There was a loud metallic clunk as the phone swallowed R. R.'s coin and the operator came on, asking for more money. Quickly R. R. searched for another dime and plopped it into the coin slot.

"There's something else," R. R. said when the operator was off. "I've checked the student files on Bartlett's friends, and one of them is left-handed. His name is Roger Peterson. What's more, and get this, Peterson went out with a girl named Sylvia Serintino just before Janowski did. See the connection? She dumped Peterson for Janowski and Peterson gets even. A love-revenge thing."

"Hold it," Conte said. "Let's not convict the kid right away." There was another silence as Conte grabbed a pad and pencil. "I'd better get some of this information down now. Bartlett's friend is Roger Peterson?"

"Yep. Left-handed Roger Peterson." R. R. gave her Roger's home aderess and telephone number.

"Listen," Conte said when she stopped writing. "I'm expecting my court order any second now. Once I've got that, I'll be pulling Bartlett's file—legally—and talking to him. Before I do, I'd like to see what other information you have. I might as well have up-to-date info, since it's available."

"We did pretty good, didn't we?"

"Never mind that," Conte said. "Just keep this left-handed business to yourself. No bulletins to friends. And that's important."

"Anything to help out."

Conte made another grumbling sound that wasn't meant to encourage R. R.'s future investigation. Then she hung up.

Inside the *Bugle* office again, R. R. settled into her chair and stared at the ceiling. She wanted to tell someone what she'd found out—what she'd figured out, really. She wanted to tell Susan, too, since she'd been a part of it all. She felt as if she were going to burst with the news, but still she did nothing. Conte wasn't fooling when she told R. R. to keep quiet. She could tell that she'd pushed the detective as far as she could. There were limits, R. R. thought. And she'd just reached hers.

Getting the name and address of the other boy had been surprisingly easy. When Wheeler went back to the school's administrative office, he'd discovered Jane Simms by herself. A quick story about having to question just one other student and Jane had looked up the information cheerfully.

After this his choice of action was automatic. His search of the building had been pretty thorough and led Wheeler to think the boys had fled. And since they knew that he had Bartlett's address, that left them only one place to go. Halihan's.

Wheeler drove across town furiously and pulled up in front of the house just as it began to snow. Sitting in the Plymouth, he scrutinized the house and yard. Everything looked quiet, so he sat back and waited.

Flecks of snow gathered on the windshield, obscuring his vision, and he had to turn on the wipers several times to insure a clear view of the sidewalk.

What if they went someplace else, he wondered. To another kid's home. To a hideout in another part of town. His fingers tightened on the steering wheel, turning his knuckles white, as he tried to shake off the new worry.

It might take some time, even all afternoon and into the evening, but eventually Halihan would come home. And when he did, Wheeler would be there.

Brian followed Sticks downstairs, his feet moving so fast that they barely made contact with the steps, to a fire door near the gym. A quick glance around and the two boys left the building and scurried across the faculty parking lot to the empty street beyond.

As they walked away from the school, Sticks said flatly, "I've decided to leave, Brian."

For some reason that didn't surprise Brian. The events of the last few days, the position he'd been forced into, all seemed to be pushing him to the same decision. Maybe running away was the answer. It was appealingly simple, he told himself. And yet it didn't sit well with Brian. As easy as it sounded, he knew he could never completely outrun Janowski's ghost or his own guilt.

Brian said, "I'm not sure it's such a good idea. I mean, you didn't beat up his daughter. And you didn't hit Janowski."

"Tell that to Wheeler," Sticks said, quickening his pace. Brian speeded up, too.

"The way I see it," Sticks continued, "everything's against me. Wheeler told me he was going to get me. And Roger's old man isn't going to let his dear son take all the blame. Even if the courts go easy on us here, I still have Michigan to deal with." He looked at Brian, his face anxious. "That's three strikes against me."

"But if you take off, they'll assume the worst. They'll blame you for everything."

Sticks didn't answer, only jammed his hands into his pockets and frowned. "It's this way. When I lived in Michigan I was always fooling around, getting into trouble, cutting school. Stuff like that. So one day, I got into a fight and leveled this kid. Nothing serious happened to him, you know." Here Sticks shrugged, shaking his head. "Nothing happened to him, but his father went ape, had me charged with aggravated assault. You'd think I'd hit the kid with an axe."

He told Brian what had followed—the police showing up at his house, being booked and brought to trial. "The judge went on and on about my rotten record, my attitude, everything. But he let me off with a suspended sentence because it was my first time." His expression changed dramatically as he recalled what happened next. "And you know what my father said to the judge? Huh? He said it'd do me some good to put me away. Can you believe that?"

Without missing a beat in his step, Sticks kicked at a chunk of ice and sent it skittering into the street. After that, his anger seemed to turn inward and brooding. As if to accent his mood, a light snow began falling, catching in his hair.

Brian could feel the weight of Sticks' dilemma, understand the narrowing of options down to the one left to him. Yet for Brian there was a difference. No matter what Wheeler or Roger's father said, how they painted the picture of what had happened, Brian would always have his parents to back him. They'd believe his story, especially if he stayed.

"What about your mother?" Brian tried. "Won't she . . ."

"She can't do anything," Sticks said. "She's okay and all, but my father pushes her around. He'd have her convinced that a year or two in a juvenile center would be just what I needed."

What else could he say, Brian wondered. He thought about getting Sticks to go back to school to talk with one of the counselors but rejected that idea. There was no guarantee that they would really help Sticks, and besides, with Wheeler so close they couldn't chance returning to the building.

They found themselves several blocks away from the school,

safely out of the detective's reach. Even so, they kept walking, heading toward the commons.

Brian said, "So how do you need me if you're leaving?"

"You'll help me?"

"I'm not for this," Brian said again. "But I'll help if I can."

"Thanks, Brian. Thanks." Sticks seemed to emerge slightly from his dark thoughts, a smile creasing his lips as he patted Brian on the shoulder. "I need some money. See, I only have seventeen dollars." He hauled a wad of one-dollar bills from his pocket and held them up. "It'll get me a train to New York but not much farther. And I figure I have to disappear completely— get to Colorado, someplace out West."

"How much?"

"A hundred?"

"What! Where am I . . ."

"Whatever you can get. Fifty. Twenty." There was no edge to Sticks' voice, no demand or threat behind his words. But something in his eyes was pleading with Brian for help. "I figure I can do odd jobs along the way for money, but I need to get started. And I'll pay you back everything. I promise."

They approached the boundary of the commons, and Brian stopped and said, "Why don't you wait at the monument while I try to round up some cash. When does the New York train leave?"

Sticks shook his head.

"Great escape plan," Brian mumbled. "Okay, you hang tough and I'll be back as soon as I can."

He left Sticks and immediately headed for his home. There was no use in going back to the school to beg from friends. Too many questions. Besides, Wheeler might be there, waiting. That left his bank account.

He had a little over two hundred dollars in his account, for emergencies his mother always reminded him. Well, this was an emergency.

He went up Temple Street, his legs picking up speed as he

thought over what he had to do during the next few hours: get his bank book—and think up a good story in case his mother was home. Then get to the bank, withdraw the money, hurry back to the commons, and put Sticks on a train. And then . . . ?

Snow was coming down steadily when Brian finally turned the corner to his street; the wind, wet and biting, crawled up his sleeves and made him shiver. A television antenna wire snapped against a house he was passing.

He came to the edge of Shendly's property and his steps slowed, thoughts about what he'd tell his mother nagging at him. He glanced up and saw the brown Plymouth waiting in front of his house less than a hundred feet away. The detective had already climbed out of the car.

There was no time to think or be afraid. Just precious seconds to move. Brian turned and bolted up and across Shendly's front lawn. The motion sent a ripping pain across his chest that made him wince and falter. He got his arms and legs working again.

"Brian, stop," Wheeler shouted. "Stop right there."

Brian remembered pulling his head down and hurling his body around the corner of his neighbor's house. He stumbled on the ground, slammed into some garbage cans, and then he was running up the side path. Frantically he searched his memory for an escape route and then remembered the hole in the hedge behind Shendly's garage. When he looked at the structure, it seemed as if it were a mile away.

"Brian!" His name was called again, but he kept on running. Then, unmistakably clear and chilling, he heard the sharp metallic click of a revolver hammer being pulled back.

The moment Wheeler saw the movement at the end of the block, his nerves jumped. It's got to be him, he thought. It's got to be the Halihan kid.

The boy was walking toward him slowly, gazing down at his feet and lost in thought. When he was two hundred feet away,

Wheeler was sure it was Halihan. Let him get closer, a voice inside his head said. He's walking right into it.

As the boy came even with the house next door, Wheeler opened the car door quietly and stepped out.

Immediately Halihan looked up, looked right at Wheeler as he'd done on Sunday at the Janowski house, though this time he was so close that Wheeler could see the confusion and fear in his eyes clearly. Then he turned and began running.

"Brian, stop." Wheeler dashed around the Plymouth, just as Halihan went across the other house's front yard, his feet tossing up large clots of snow as they dug in and gained speed. Wheeler shouted, "Stop right there."

Get him. Get him, the voice screamed. Don't let him get away again.

He followed the boy's tracks across the yard. From ahead, around the corner of the house, a deafening clatter of metal came back to Wheeler, and when he got there he found the path strewn with cans and garbage. The boy was almost to the backyard.

This proves it, the voice insisted. There's no doubt.

"Stop!" Wheeler commanded. "Brian, stop."

He leaped a garbage can, his left hand undoing the safety snap of his holster, while his right hand fumbled for the handle. He skidded to a halt on the icy path, his weapon snapping level with his eye.

He's guilty. They're all guilty. He steadied his revolver so it pointed at the base of the boy's skull. Guilty, the voice chanted again and again. Guilty. Then Wheeler's thumb found the hammer and cocked it into firing position. Guilty . . .

14

*B*rian leaped a small ornamental hedge at the back of Shendly's house and ran straight through the remains of the old man's last tomato crop. He had hunched forward a second before, waiting for the terrible impact of a bullet, and his running was awkward.

Don't stop. Don't listen, he told himself as he squeezed between the old garage and the massive pine hedge. If he remembered correctly, the opening in the hedge was just a few feet up and led into the adjoining yard.

He paused a second but heard no shouts. No footsteps. This confused him, made him wonder if Wheeler had anticipated his thinking and gone to head him off. He rejected this idea, telling himself not to be trapped by his fear.

He pushed through the opening, the frozen nettles biting into his hands and face. The yard he entered was flat and without fences or shrubs, just an open avenue to the street beyond, with no people in sight.

He ran down the driveway, a dog inside the house barking madly, but no other challenges being flung at him. Once across the street, he could disappear into the maze of backyards, alleys, and driveways he'd known from childhood. His running slowed momentarily as he recalled the click of the revolver's hammer. Why hadn't a shot been fired? And why hadn't Wheeler come after him?

His pace quickened again. He had no time to waste thinking of these things. He had only precious seconds to escape.

The boy was only a hundred or so feet away and an easy target. Wheeler's left hand came up and wrapped around the other, steadying the revolver, helping him to concentrate.

He felt the cold metal of the handle, the springed resistance of the trigger. The thumb holding the hammer in check twitched imperceptibly, seemed to nag at Wheeler to act. . . . It was an instant when the voice inside him was subdued and the reality of the moment took over. He recalled the last time he'd drawn his weapon—and in that second of hesitation, Brian vanished behind the garage.

Everything in Wheeler told him to give chase. The boy only had a short lead and was probably too scared to think clearly. He could still catch him. Instead, Wheeler lowered the revolver and put it back into his holster carefully, wiping the sweat from his palm after that.

Quickly he checked the surrounding houses to see if anyone had been watching. The windows stared back at him, empty. Yet even knowing there were no witnesses didn't ease the embarrassment or self-doubt. He'd almost done it again, he realized. He'd lost control and come within a finger's movement of letting his well-trained reflexes dictate his actions.

He went to the garage, though he wasn't surprised to find the space between it and the hedge empty. He was relieved, actually.

He turned to go back to the Plymouth and found an old, white-haired man dressed in dungarees and floppy rubber boots clomping down the back stairs.

"What's all the racket about out here?" the man demanded. "And who the hell are you, busting into my yard?" He squinted his eyes and gave Wheeler a hard, thorough looking over. "Huh? Say something."

"Police," Wheeler replied quietly. He went up the side path toward the front, an odd, numb feeling invading his body.

"Police, huh? Well, what's going on, anyway?" Mr. Shendly

asked, trailing Wheeler by a few steps. He caught sight of the mess on the side of his house. "Holy b'jeepers, look at this. You guys think you can charge around anywhere, don't you? Let me tell you something. . . ."

Wheeler stepped over the garbage and headed for his car.

"Aren't you even going to help clean this mess up?" Shendly snorted angrily and kicked a lid. "I'm going to have a little talk with one of your bosses, sonny. You wait and see. Think you own the place 'cause you got a tin badge. I'll show you."

Inside the Plymouth, Wheeler let the windshield wipers whoosh back and forth lazily for a few minutes. The snow was coming down heavier now, but it was still light and powdery and easily swept aside by the blades.

Once again his brain began to suggest a course of action—circle the block, keep moving along the streets in the area, and the boy was bound to make a blunder. Or he could go to Bartlett's house. Since the boys had split up, it was possible that Bartlett had gone home, seeking its familiar safety. But as each idea came to him, he rejected it.

He got the car moving finally, the tires slipping through the layer of fresh snow on the road. Suddenly he wanted to get away from it all.

For Brian, the next twenty minutes sped by in a blur. He had little sense of direction at first—just a frantic need to get away from the detective. Then, as his head cleared, he found himself several blocks away and decided to go back to the commons.

At the monument, Brian found Sticks pacing restlessly in the small area, the ground littered with half-smoked stubs of cigarettes.

"How'd it go?" Sticks asked.

Brian shook his head and plopped down on the cold marble step to catch his breath. "He was waiting for me," Brian said. "He knows about both of us now."

Sticks slumped down next to Brian and leaned his head back

164

so the flakes of snow that managed to get through the tangle of pine branches above landed on his face. The cool wetness seemed to make him feel calmer. At last he said, "I guess I'll just go to New York with what I've got. I can't hang around here for much longer."

"It won't work," Brian said. He felt an obligation to help Sticks, to make sure that he got away cleanly. "It won't take him very long to figure out where you went, and without money he'll be on you in no time."

"It's all I can do."

Sticks rose and began bouncing around to warm his legs and feet. Before Friday that action would have made Brian nervous; now it just set a rhythm for his thinking. "There's still Amy," Brian said a few minutes later. "Maybe I can get some money from her."

"You think so? You think she'd help?"

Brian nodded. "But we can't chance going back to school," he said, "so we're going to have to sit tight til school's out."

"No problem."

Sticks sat next to Brian and pulled out a cigarette. Before he'd finished smoking it, he'd checked his watch several times, jumped to his feet, paced a little, and sat down again. When he ran out of cigarettes thirty minutes after this, Sticks filled the time by muttering about the cold.

Brian let Sticks burn up his nervous energy without response, preferring to close his eyes and wait quietly. He wondered what Wheeler was up to, imagined him questioning his mother or cruising the streets patiently, eyes alert. Then, through these thoughts, Brian heard a church bell strike three times.

"I guess this is it," Brian said, rising and shaking the cold from his body.

"Yeah," Sticks grunted solemnly.

Before leaving the safety of the monument, Brian poked his head out and scanned the open area. A few cars moved through the falling snow; a few people labored up the sidewalk—but there was no sign of Wheeler.

"If that detective comes after us," Brian said, turning to Sticks, "just run and don't stop. He can only get one of us and I'll make sure it's me."

Sticks nodded.

They walked across the commons and moved along the streets as quickly as possible without running or drawing attention to themselves. Speed was important, Brian realized. If they wanted to stay ahead of Wheeler, they had to move quickly. About a block from Amy's, Brian told Sticks to wait.

"Here," he said, handing Sticks the eleven dollars he had on him. "If he's waiting for me at Amy's . . ." He shrugged, not bothering to finish the sentence. "I'll try to be back in a few minutes."

"Good luck."

As Brian moved closer to Amy's house, he was able to see the effects of the snow for the first time. The uniform, unblemished covering imposed a peacefulness on the block. He could imagine people inside their warm houses, watching television or reading, free of the worries Brian had. No one else would help Sticks; no one else would believe his innocence. He had to help him.

He rang the doorbell, and a second later Amy stuck her head out. "Ah, hi," she said, after an instant of confusion. "I wasn't . . . you know . . ."

"I guess I did bomb in on you."

"That's okay, though," she said, opening the door and smiling at him. She was wearing a baggy pair of jeans and big puff-ball slippers trimmed with pink edging. "Come in." She took Brian's arm and gently tugged him inside the enclosed porch. "I was worried about you. After history class"—she seemed embarrassed at having brought it up—"I tried to find you after lunch but couldn't."

"I had to help a friend out. He's in trouble. That's why I'm here."

166

"Can you stay a while?"

Brian motioned over his shoulder with his thumb. "My friend's waiting for me. I can't. Not today, anyway."

"Amy, is anyone there?" Amy's mother called from somewhere inside the house.

"It's Brian," Amy hollered back in a way that also said they wanted to be alone. She closed the door and looked thoughtful. "Let's see. You can't stay very long. Someone's waiting for you outside. If I have any brain matter working, that means you want some sort of favor. Right?"

"Yep," he said. "I need some money."

"Money!" It came out as a surprised yelp, which quickly turned to laughter. "You're some smooth operator."

"I wouldn't ask if it wasn't important."

"I'm only kidding, Brian. If you need money and I have any, it's yours." She still had hold of Brian, so she pulled him into the living room and parked him on the sofa. Then she asked, "How much?"

"Fifty dollars." He saw her eyes widen in surprise and added, "It's not for me. It's for . . ."

"I know, your friend." She wanted to ask him some questions, find out if there was anything else she could do. She could tell that something was troubling him deeply—the way he talked, the way his eyes kept moving around and never settled on anything for very long. Still, she sensed that this wasn't the time. She said, "Stay put and I'll see what I can find."

She ran upstairs and Brian could hear her opening and closing dresser drawers, digging around hurriedly. It wasn't long before she came marching downstairs, clutching some bills and change in her hand.

"I could only find twenty-seven sixty," she said, giving it to Brian. "It's not much."

"Terrific." He jammed it into his pocket and inched toward the door. "He's . . ."

"Waiting."

"Yeah."

"Can you call me tonight?"

"I'll try," he said, pulling open the front door and stepping out onto the porch. "I really will."

"I believe you," she said. And he went down the stairs and into the swirling snow.

Wheeler drove the entire length of Edgewater, then made a series of turns, regulating the speed of the car so that it didn't stall. The light began to fade, and he snapped the headlights on, the yellow beam cutting through the snow.

The simple act of driving, of maneuvering over the slippery road, shifting his foot from accelerator to brake and back to the accelerator, forced him to settle down. To think.

Weisinski had been right: he was too close to the case. What's more, he'd pushed everybody too far, taken advantage of them—Hobart, Gail, the principal of the school. Even Susan. He'd used them to get at the boys. And now that he had, he wasn't sure what it had gotten him.

A quiet sadness settled over him as he realized he'd fallen into the worst trap his power as a cop offered—he'd not only set out to find the kids responsible for Janowski's death; he'd judged them as well. His only consolation was that this time he hadn't been able to carry out the sentence.

When he found himself cruising through a small shopping area, he pulled over to the curb and killed the engine. To his right, he saw a butcher shop with a sign in the window that read: Don't Let Thanksgiving Go to the Birds—Celebrate with Beef. Lights twinkled on and off, announcing the holiday's arrival. Wheeler was surprised that it was only ten days away.

Well, the least he could do now was to phone the station and tell them what he'd discovered about Bartlett and Halihan. And tell what he'd done to get the information. He located a pay phone, put his coins in, and when the desk sergeant answered, he asked for Hobart.

15

As soon as Brian and Sticks got to the train station, Brian went inside and bought a ticket for New York on the four-thirty Expressliner. Then he rejoined Sticks outside on the platform next to the tracks and waited.

When the train was twenty minutes late, Brian found himself growing nervous, fidgety. He felt his entire body tightening. Given enough time, Wheeler would be on them. Sticks didn't say anything, but his eyes revealed the same concern.

"Won't be long now," Brian said, more as a wish than a guarantee. He checked the shadows for Wheeler.

"Must be the snow," Sticks added. Brian could barely hear his friend's words over the sound of the gusting wind. Sticks leaned out and looked up the tracks. "I don't want you to get into any trouble for helping me," he said when he'd turned back to face Brian.

Brian shrugged.

"I mean it. If you think it would help, I'll write to the cops and explain everything. Or I'll call somebody."

"I'll do okay," Brian said. And he believed it, too.

A sharp snap of wind struck the platform, whipped around the building, and threw snow up into Brian's face. A bell on the platform shrilled.

"Train's coming," Brian said. Just then the station door opened and people came out onto the platform, huddling in a protective clump a few feet away from the two boys. A train horn sounded; the heavy rumble of the tracks shook the platform.

169

"I guess this is it," Sticks said.

Brian almost responded with "You don't have to go, you know," but he knew that wasn't true. Wheeler wouldn't have hunted them so relentlessly unless he expected to prosecute to the fullest. And Sticks had no one to turn to for help, no one to defend him. Brian said simply, "Yep. This is it."

The big diesel rolled past the boys, metal brakes screeching the Expressliner to a halt. It was a momentary stop in the train's journey, a pause to let three people off and take on eight.

Brian clapped Sticks on the back. "Well, good luck and all that."

"You think I'd be here if I had any sort of luck?" Sticks joked, a silly grin appearing. When Brian didn't smile, Sticks said, "Hey, it's not as if I just died or anything. I'll do okay, you wait and see. This is probably the smartest thing I've ever done."

"Take care," Brian said. "And don't forget to buy some warm clothes. You'll freeze your butt off in that leather jacket."

"Thanks again, Brian. For everything."

"Just don't do anything stupid," Brian called after him as Sticks climbed the high steps of the passenger car and disappeared inside.

Brian stood on the platform as the other passengers boarded. Sticks located a seat near a window, and after peering out at Brian and waving, he settled back.

He looks safe in there, Brian thought. There was a fleeting wish on Brian's part to join Sticks, to leave Edgewater and everything behind—but the train horn blasted the idea from his head. It was right for Sticks, but not for him. A conductor called "Clear!" and then the train began inching from the station. Brian watched it recede down the tracks, the yellow and red running lights growing smaller and smaller, the horn's wail being swallowed by the night.

Wheeler walked across the front yard, enjoying the cold, clean smell of the air and the intense quiet the snow seemed to impose on the neighborhood. It was as if it were all new to him.

Even his thought pattern had altered, calmed. The vividness of Janowski lying dead in the park had faded, to be replaced by an image with less definition, as if seen from a greater distance. And his remembrance of Mr. and Mrs. Janowski also seemed less immediate and compelling.

Hobart's news had something to do with this. It seemed that Conte had gone to Truman that afternoon to question Bartlett, but when he couldn't be located, she'd descended on a couple of his friends. After some very carefully chosen words—about the fingerprints the police had and their knowledge that a left-hander was responsible—plus some gentle threats, one of the boys, Alan Kendall, had told Conte everything, including his taking part in Susan's attack. When confronted with this, the second friend, Roger Peterson, buckled immediately, admitting his part in all of it.

So it was over, Wheeler thought. All they had to do now was locate Bartlett and Halihan and press formal charges for all four: for Peterson, two counts of aggravated assault and maybe even a third-degree manslaughter charge; one count of aggravated assault for Kendall. The other two—Bartlett and Halihan—would be charged with withholding information about a felony. And since the death appeared to be unpremeditated, the judge would probably kick them all out of court and place them with a juvenile counselor. It was simple—for everyone but Wheeler.

As soon as he had the front door open, Susan came bounding across the living room to him and threw her arms around his waist.

"Isn't it great," she shouted. "About catching the kids who killed Janowski. And it was all R. R.'s doing . . . and yours, too, of course."

"I just heard the news myself," Wheeler said. Gail appeared at the door to the utility room, clutching a pair of pliers. "I guess our patient here has made a miraculous recovery," he added, nodding in Susan's direction.

"The great thing," Susan went on excitedly, "is that R. R. just read the reports and figured it out. It was right in front of her. And guess what. Detective Conte said we could write a story about it since the case is closed."

"Now she wants to be an investigative reporter," Gail sighed. She still seemed tired, but her anger had dissipated, overcome no doubt by Susan's enthusiasm. "I'm not sure I can handle the two of you at the same time," she said good-naturedly.

"R. R. and I are going to work on the story together," Susan continued. "Then when we're finished we're going to do another story about . . ."

"No more police cases, I hope," Wheeler said firmly.

"No. Detective Conte said this one story was it." She tugged at his arm, pulling him into the kitchen. Gail followed. "See, I've been working on a list. We're going to start with the city council. They've been up to some pretty funny stuff lately."

"Those poor people don't know what they're in for," Wheeler said.

As Susan detailed all her plans, Wheeler was able to study Gail. She seemed genuinely pleased with Susan's new interest; the corners of her lips were curled slightly in amusement and showed no trace of the previous tension. Or fear. He wouldn't tell her just now. He'd wait till Susan was asleep.

"Don't make any rash decisions," Hobart had told him— commanded him—when they'd spoken earlier. "We all do stupid things once in a while, Bob, and you're no different, hear?" Hobart was the Poppa Bear watching over his clan. "Don't you think I've gone over the edge a few times myself? And nothing really happened, did it? You pushed your way around a little, but *nothing happened*."

Not this time, Wheeler thought. But he still had the memory of Willy Jackson to live with, as well as the vision of his revolver aimed at Halihan's back. He'd come too close to just let it ride by.

172